First published in Great Britain in 2010 by Comma Press
www.commapress.co.uk

The right of the authors and translators to be identified has been asserted in accordance
with the Copyright Designs and Patent Act 1988.

'Crocus or Drowsy Blossom' first appeared in *Ogleden Sonra Ask* by Nedim Gürsel (Dogan
Egmond Yayincilik, 2002). 'A Couple of People' first appeared in the anthology *Timeout
Istanbul Hikayeleri* (Ajans Medya, 2007). 'The Well' first appeared in *Tas Hucre* by Türker
Armaner (Metis, 2000). 'A Question' first appeared in *Kisa Omurlu Acelyalar* by Müge İplikçi
(Everest Yayinlari, 2009). 'Out of Reach' first appeared in *Parcali Asklar* by Gönül Kıvılcım
(Everest Yayinlari, 2004). 'Marked in Writing' first appeared in *On uc Buyulu Oyku* by Murat
Gülsoy (Can Yayinlari, 2002). 'The Intersection' first appeared in *Yaz Evi* by Mehmet
Zaman Saçlıoğlu (Is Bankasi Yayinlari, 2002). 'Istanbul, Your Eyes are Black' first appeared
in *Cumhuriyet Gazetesi* by Karin Karakaşlı (Cumhuriyet Gazetesi, 2006). 'I Did Not Kill
Monsieur Moise' first appeared in *Madam Floris Donmeyebilir* by Mario Levi (Dogan
Egmond Yayincilik, 2006). 'Panther' first appeared in *Tanri Kimseyi Duymuyor* by Özen Yula
(Yapi Kredi Yayincilik, 2005).

A CIP catalogue record of this book is available from the British Library.

Lines taken from 'The Wasteland: III. The Fire Sermon' in SELECTED POEMS by T.S
Eliot (Faber and Faber, 1948), p59, line 220. Reprinted by permission.

ISBN 1905583311
ISBN-13   978 1905583324

LOTTERY FUNDED

The publisher gratefully acknowledges assistance from Arts Council England.
This book has been published with the support of the Ministry of Culture and Tourism
of the Republic of Turkey within the framework of the TEDA Project.

This anthology was produced in collaboration with the British Council, which in 2010
celebrates the 70th anniversary of its presence in Turkey promoting cultural relations
with the United Kingdom.

Set in Bembo 11/13 by David Eckersall
Printed and bound in England by SRP Ltd, Exeter

THE BOOK OF ISTANBUL

A City in Short Fiction

Edited by
Jim Hinks &
Gul Turner

Contents

Introduction

THIS ANTHOLOGY INTRODUCES ten writers who, while not widely published in English translation, are considered in Turkey to be leading exponents of the short form. Their stories, set in and around Istanbul, together make for a kind of literary tour of the city's notable districts and environs, pausing here and there to contemplate the historical events that have forged the modern-day metropolis. Set in the present, they also have an eye on the past; each has something to say about the city's evolution during the past seventy years.

Istanbul spans Asia and Europe, dissevered by the Bosphorus Strait. The noble old districts that line each side are – naturally enough – built facing the shore, and so the predominant view, wherever one stands, is of the other side. On the European shore, looking across the water, one is acutely aware of being at the frontier of Asia. On the Anatolian side, one contemplates the West. As such, one might either regard Istanbul as uniting the two continents – a bridging point between the traditions, religions and cultures of East and West – or torn, irreconcilably, between them.

This tension - between European and Asian influence – is discernable in the stories collected here. Yula, Kıvılcım and Gülsoy, for example, recall a verbose, playful, Arabic tradition that favours elevating the voice, spinning a tale, incorporating mythical allusions, deferring the dramatic crux of the story in favour of asides and digressions. But there are also traces of European influence: echoes in the stories of Kaygusuz and Armaner of de Maupassant and Kafka. If pushed to identify a common characteristic, it's perhaps the latitude the Turkish language permits its authors to interject a fleeting metaphor or image or passing thought into the narrative without breaking stride, the tendency to adroitly step from one subject to another and back again all within the same sentence. It seems all the more arresting when one's palate is attuned to modern English and American short stories, which often favour a unity of tone prohibitive of sudden delights and surprises.

Since 1965, the population of Istanbul has increased from around one and a half million people to over thirteen million people. Though in part due to the expansion of municipal boundaries, the swallowing up of neighbouring towns (indeed, centuries ago, even many of Istanbul's central districts, including Galata on the European side, and Üsküdar and Kadıköy on the Asian side, were considered distinct cities), the statistic also reflects huge migration to the metropolis. It's a city of newcomers, a place in which most people are aware that they've arrived from elsewhere, or that their parents have, or their grandparents. The narrator of Sema Kaygusuz's story 'A Couple of People' contemplates that people in Istanbul don't live in the 'real' city, but rather its inhabitants, "play out old memories of distant homelands […] This is why the Istanbul landscape is actually just an allusion to somewhere else. The joyful mourning of what has been lost is being performed with this site as a backdrop."

For all that it's the original 'melting pot' city – a place where for centuries various ethnic groups harmoniously lived side-by-side – in the past seventy years Istanbul has seen its fair share of conflict, with purges, expulsions and persecutions, on grounds of both ethnicity and political association. A number of these events are either specifically mentioned, or implicitly alluded to, in the stories in this anthology.

Notable among these are the 'Varlık Vergisi' (Capital Tax) of 1942, a one-off tax which, in response to supposed war-profiteering by minority owned businesses, levied a higher – and often confiscatory tariff – on non-Muslims, resulting in severe hardship or exile for many of Istanbul's Armenian, Greek Orthodox and Jewish inhabitants. Although the tax was soon repealed, the situation for ethnic minorities was to worsen during the 1955 Cyprus crisis, when riots in Istanbul, in response to reports of a bomb plot against Ataturk's birthplace in Thessaloniki, Greece, targeted the ethnic Greek population (as described in Karin Karakaşlı's 'Istanbul Your Eyes Are Black').

Successive coups d'etat (in 1960, 1971 and 1980), precipitated variously by military concern over the reversal of Ataturk's secular reforms, and civil unrest at economic hardship, resulted in retaliatory persecutions of supposed agitators on both the left and right of the political spectrum. The legacy of these struggles is ubiquitous in Turkey, and most explicitly discussed here in the stories of Turker Armaner and Nedim Gürsel (Gürsel himself went into exile following the 1971 coup, and again in 1980).

More recently, heated public debate about the incursion – or prohibition – of religion in state institutions, within a largely Muslim nation founded on Kemalist secular principles, has expanded. Muge Iplikci's story, 'A Question', reflects several high-profile court cases concerning the wearing of the hijab in secular contexts. While the ban on the hijab in universities was officially relaxed in 2008, debate continues over the intersection of secular and religious traditions within Turkish society.

Twentieth century struggles have left their mark. Some of the characters within these pages exhibit a kind of instinctive guardedness, a reticence about sharing personal information – about where they come from, or what they believe in – in the public realm. There's something clandestine about them. And when their private lives are rent open, the consequences can be disastrous.

As such, many of these stories reach their dramatic apex when the security of domestic space is compromised - or when peculiarly private people cross the threshold into an uncaring city. It's a trope that occurs again and again. These writers use common, municipal space – places that all *Istanbullu* would recognise – as a crucible in which their characters' hopes and insecurities are laid bare: in cafés and bars, in marketplaces and squares, on benches overlooking the Bosphorus.

Likewise, many of the stories themselves masquerade as something else. They purport to be one thing, when in fact, underneath, something quite different lurks. There are stories that use the framework of a traditional romance to keep the memory of an injustice alive. Stories that focus on the personal, the domestic, to celebrate the wider struggles of a persecuted minority, or to question class prejudice.

Some of the authors in this anthology have themselves endured persecution – through the courts or in the press – for their work. Nedim Gürsel faced trial in 2009 on the charge of 'denigrating religious values' after the publication of his novel *The Daughters of Allah,* and Ozen Yula was recently subjected to a ferocious press campaign to close his play *Lick but Don't Swallow.* It's mistaken to characterise Turkish society as fundamentalist or intolerant. It's not. The extreme actions of a few naturally attract the most international press attention. And yet at the same time, it's worth noting that several of these authors have put their liberty and livelihood at stake in order to publish their work, to tell their story of Istanbul.

Jim Hinks, October 2010.

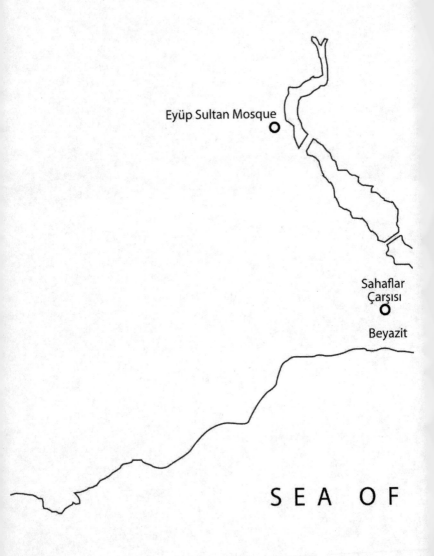

Eyüp Sultan Mosque

Sahaflar
Çarşısı

Beyazit

S E A   O F

2 mi
2 km

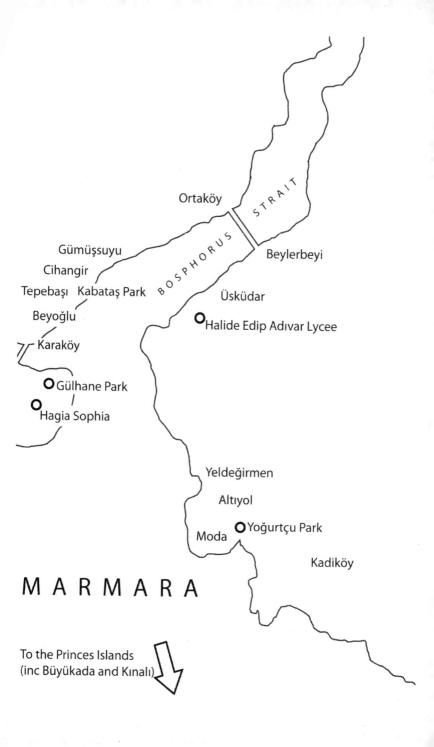

Crocus,
or Drowsy Blossom

Nedim Gürsel

I DON'T RECALL exactly when and where I met Çiğdem. And this, frankly, makes me a little uneasy. I'm not about to say that my memory is fading; I'm not old enough yet. Besides, what does it mean to be old? The days might feel shorter, but if your inner child has not come of age, if time continues to flow unhurriedly and the possibility of dying in bed still seems remote, who is to argue that you've grown old? By dying in bed, I'm of course referring to the inevitable end that we commonly ascribe to fate, not to the little death experienced with a woman. The source of my unease is different. I'm afraid my memory is getting increasingly selective. At times I'll remember the smallest, the most inconsequential detail, but then the memories of women I once knew well, those objects of passionate lovemaking – during long or brief affairs, or even just one night stands – seem ever more evaporating. Imagine ships travelling in the fog. You can make out a mast here, red and green lights there, or a propeller in the frothy sea. If the ships didn't sound off their foghorns, they might collide and sink at any moment. The women in my memory are like those ships in the fog – disjointed bits and pieces, indistinct. Çiğdem, too, is one of them. Neither the most beautiful nor the most faithful. Certainly among the wildest. Of course I am able to say this only in hindsight, after years of never getting in touch. I suppose I wasn't the most faithful either.

If I can't recall when and where I met Çiğdem, I think it's because we never sought each other out after the break-up. Frankly, I didn't want to see her again. She had to remain faded in my mind, muted, lost among thoughts. Except for the memory of her hands, her reckless driving, and an Istanbul afternoon at a table by the Bosphorus, the lovely carnations on the table, their dizzying scent. I was a first-year student at the university. Nowadays, if someone were to ask me about the state of affairs at the time, I'd summarize it like this:

When the generals at the Joint Command finished listening to Beethoven and issued their memorandum, the plump and democratic Prime Minister picked up his hat and left; a new Government from within the chain-of-command was summoned to replace the one forced to resign; intellectuals, workers, leftist party leaders were imprisoned – while some went into hiding – and the revolutionary youth began dying on the mountains and the gallows. After the factories and the shipyards, the nation's universities, too, were occupied like they were enemy positions, and the dissenters were pacified whether by caning or by interrogation. Those whom the terror overlooked found refuge in foreign countries. There, after the many friendships - or bastardries - tested by fire and fury, they still dream of the day they shall overcome.

So in this environment, I must have met Çiğdem. Perhaps in an auditorium where students from different years took classes together, perhaps at the cafeteria, or perhaps in one of the taverns where circles of friends gathered. The point is, because our relationship – the misborn child of March 12[1] – never involved lovemaking in the true sense of the term (I trust I don't need to explain what I mean by 'true sense'), settings gain particular significance among my memories of her. More precisely, cars. One car in particular. The Anadol – the pride and glory of the regime in those years.

1. March 12 – The date of the military coup of 1971

CROCUS

Obviously Çiğdem didn't brag about owning a car made in Turkey. She was actually a modest, timid girl, perhaps because she wasn't beautiful or because her brother was in prison. She was affectionate, it's true, but she wasn't particularly pretty. Slightly bowlegged, she sort of waddled, and couldn't walk at all when she wore high-heels. She was the daughter of a civil servant. The father had purchased the car with his retirement bonus. When he died, the car was passed on to her brother, and when the martial law rounded him up, to Çiğdem. She and her mother lived in a small flat. I never saw their home and knew it only from Çiğdem's descriptions. Two bedrooms and a living room, as melancholy as herself. Not once did I pick up my sweetheart or drop her off at her home.

Throughout our time together, she came in her car to pick me up at my mother's home. Unremarkably, I, too, lived with my mother. Student dorms in those days were under police occupation; most of our university friends were either under surveillance or in prison, and some, frightened by the events, had returned to their hometowns. Istanbul was suddenly deserted. Or so it seemed to us. In those years, we thought the city consisted of nothing else but the streets we walked, the neighbourhoods we visited, the coffeehouses and taverns we gathered in. Say, Çınaraltı cafe at the entrance of the second-hand book bazaar, Paradise Beer Garden in Cihangir, or maybe Park Hotel and the cheap taverns along the Bosphorus. The more we thought about the friends who left us young, the lonelier we felt. We felt hopeless and pessimistic. In this twenty-somethings' Istanbul, we were like lost migratory birds.

There was also something different about Çiğdem's disposition, not just her walk. If you ask me, 'What was it?' I would now respond without a moment's hesitation, 'timid yet daring,' but at the time I would've had no idea what that meant. Her gaze was childlike, naïve, guileless. Her hair, her eyes, even her lips were dark, as dark as black, a bit off-putting.

3

Her hands were the most beautiful – more beautiful than the hands of any woman I've known before or, for that matter, since. You'd swear she was not created of Adam's rib. It was as though God on the ceiling of the Sistine Chapel had reached down from among the angels and given life not to Adam but to Çiğdem; from the tip of that limp finger, life had passed into her body. That's why she had elongated fingers, soft palms, slender wrists.

When we first met, I recall we exchanged greetings without shaking hands. I discovered her hands' talent much later; as for their beauty, I first noticed that during a dinner just for two. As she cut the meat on her plate, she held the knife's handle as if it were a pen, and her movements were swift and delicate, like those of a violin virtuoso. Were we at The Captain's or Nazmi's Place in Arnavutköy? Nazmi's Place had to have been closed for some time; that unsightly apartment building was probably beginning to rise from its garden. Then we must have been at The Captain's. The 'staked road' had not been built yet. I recall we were sitting at a table by the sea. Can you imagine? You go out with your girlfriend for a leisurely, intimate dinner by the sea, and the next time you go back, the restaurant is not where you left it. No, it hasn't moved elsewhere; its setting is slightly altered, that's all. The place is the same, the tables, too, are the same. But now there is a causeway suspended on big wooden stakes in front of the restaurant – yes, you heard it right – and you watch a deluge of cars sending tremors through the wooden frames of the yalıs along the Bosphorus, at the foot of the hills gnawed by concrete structures. The traffic has loosened up and so have the nerves. No one is shouting or screaming on account of gridlocks; taxi and dolmuş drivers are happy. The sliver of the sea, still visible between land and causeway, has turned into a garbage dump. The table where you once sat together – drowsily gazing at the moon's reflection on the water – is shaking with the rumble of trucks and public buses. Further out, on the corner where the shore and the 'staked road' converge, the sea is covered with plastic bottles and vegetable waste. Oil stains glisten in the seven colors of the sun; tattered rags that somehow haven't sunk to the bottom float listlessly. Each time the waters rise, the waste is swept onto the causeway. Anyway, maybe we didn't meet at The Captain's when we went there with friends, but I am certain the two of us had dinner there. Afterwards, Çiğdem gave me a ride back to my house – our dark flat that never saw the sunlight, near Çukurbostan. Even after we left the causeway and dived into the streets of Ortaköy, we were driving very fast. We didn't wear seatbelts back then. I recall being terrified. I asked Çiğdem to slow down a bit, but she didn't seem to care. I remember sticking my head out of the car window, trying to sober up with the wind. Did I say, to sober up? It would be more accurate to say, to cool off. That particular summer, as if the martial law wasn't enough, the city was assaulted by an unbearable heat wave and a plague of hungry worms. Even the mulberry tree in Çukurbostan under which we used to lay a kilim[2] and sit, could not provide relief from the sun; the worms had eaten all its leaves. Perhaps my love was driving fast so she could drop me off and get herself home before the start of the curfew. Çiğdem! Çiğdem! Just as I did in your car, while you treated me to moments of pleasure and panic, now, too, I can repeat your name endlessly. By giving each syllable its due, by adding extra stress on 'm', the way you floored the gas pedal. But I won't tease you by calling you, Çiğden![3] Because I probably want to avoid the allusion to the 'raw meat' that turns my early morning dreams to nightmares; or because I'm full of remorse for having called you Çiğden so many times.

But Çiğdem didn't seem to mind. Just a dark grin formed across her small mouth, revealing her white teeth. I neglected to say that Çiğdem had a slight overbite, which lent her a distinct appeal. As if she was ready to bite into an apple

2. Kilim - a flat tapestry-woven carpet or rug.
3. Çiğden – Suggesting eating something raw (çiğ).

or a man's flesh at any time. Çiğdem! My daring lover! Yes, for a while – a brief while, and perhaps because of the curfews – I loved her passionately; although I wasn't madly in love, I was, how shall I put it, awestruck. As soon as Nihat Erim's Operation Sledgehammer[4] started – had he not fallen to a terrorist bullet, I would have used his nickname, 'Bald Nihat' – I escaped to Paris, leaving everything behind, including my love. Many years passed since. One day, when I thought I had forgotten Çiğdem, a criminal incident – actually, it was a murder, a horrific murder, but I am speaking euphemistically perhaps to legitimize the carnivore's instinct that my lover used to arouse in me, in any case, this criminal incident – led me to remember Çiğdem.

At the Sorbonne, a Japanese student studying Kawabata for his doctorate in comparative literature – we were in a seminar together although we never spoke, and besides, he was quiet and withdrawn, a short man, quite possibly a dwarf – killed his Dutch girlfriend with a long-range rifle. For reasons unknown, he shot her while she was sitting next to him, chopped her to pieces, put them in the freezer and ate them raw, with knife and fork, one piece per meal, until all were gone. Try to picture a young man from the Far East eating his girlfriend in the small kitchen of his studio apartment in a garret. His napkin is tucked in his collar, he has opened a bottle of red wine, on his plate is a piece of meat found only at the most deluxe French restaurants, barely cooked, just passed over a flame and served 'bleu'; the man is eating with great appetite – no, let me call it what it is – lustfully. During his deposition at the police station, the Japanese student said that he ate his Dutch girlfriend because he loved her very much. He loved her to death, but she was oblivious. In fact, lately, she had started acting aloof, even making fun of his dwarf body. After all, she was tall and shapely, she'd had plenty of protein, no doubt on account of

4. Nihat Erim – Prime Minister for fourteen months in 1971-72; assassinated in 1980.

6

the bounteous Dutch cows' milk she was fed as a baby. As for the Japanese, the future doctor (of literature, that is) wasn't one to swallow his pride and seek consolation among the prostitutes, was he? He, too, had dreams, moments when he forgot that he was short. He, too, was human, loved humanity – certainly enough to eat his own kind. He committed the deed because he wanted to become one with his beloved, to absorb her body, to distill it, in his body. Not because he was evil. After all, eating one's beloved – or enemy – was in the nature of being human.

The court found him not guilty by reason of insanity and sent the murderer to the asylum rather than the prison. Once there, he became rich by writing books that described in detail how he ate his beloved. After a while, he was repatriated to his own country. He continues to write best-sellers, while also making pornographic movies on the side. Recently I saw one of the movie posters. The Japanese porn-star was lying in bed naked, looking lovely and innocent like a sleeping baby. Two full-figured women knelt next to him. Both naked, too. They were holding knives and forks. Another time, I read in a newspaper that a miniature replica of the Eiffel Tower was built in front of his house, and the entrance to the restaurant next door boasted in French, 'la viande est bonne.' I don't want to be misunderstood. Of course I never fantasized about eating Çiğdem. Not once. Although I sometimes called her 'Çiğden' to tease her, and although 'eating' or 'eating each other,' in the masculine argot means 'kissing,' or even further, 'tasting each other with the mouth,' I believe I am sane enough to know the consequences of the actual deed. In this instance, I am merely concerned with my girlfriend's name. Besides, as I already mentioned, she was not a shapely woman, nowhere near buxom. Fragile, petite. A twig, as they say. Still, she always made me think of raw meat. I wanted to sink my teeth into her name, roll it around my mouth, chew it well, and I felt ashamed whenever, all of a sudden, in the most unexpected time or place – for instance at The Captain's – this desire would envelop my entire being like an irresistible urge.

Yes, I had forgotten Çiğdem in that paradise of women called Paris. And had the Japanese student not committed that horrific murder, I probably would not have remembered her. But why am I calling this murderer 'a student'? Perhaps because I found his motivation as noble as Raskolnikov or because he was no longer a murderer but a famous author and porn-star.

Almost every day, Çiğdem came to pick me up with her car. We had both abandoned our studies. And our circle of friends. Besides, there was hardly anyone left to talk with. Our closest friends were either in prison or in exile. And maybe Çiğdem came to me every day because she couldn't visit her brother in prison and bring him 'neither a box of eggs nor a pair of woollen socks,' in the words of the revolutionary poet we read in those days. But we were two lovers, not siblings. We would start drinking in the car, and continue at a shabby tavern. We did go to nicer restaurants every so often, but as poor as we were, we had to seek out the cheap ones. Köprüaltı, for instance. Or the moonshiner taverns. Or The Arab's Place in Üsküdar, where we'd get drunk sitting by the window that opened to the most beautiful scenery in the city. Afterwards: *Carry us away, Istanbul!* Shoreline boulevards, narrow streets, up and down the two coasts, night after night, high on speed and alcohol.

Back in those days, people who knew cars considered the Anadol's bodywork useless. If your car was the homemade Anadol, then it was extremely unsafe to park it in a field or a pasture. A horse or a donkey grazing there – still worse, livestock like, say, an ox or a horned buffalo – could just chomp or ram into the fibreglass body. One day, a dawdler yelled while we drove by, 'I'll eat your car, sister!' 'If he knew your name, he'd want to eat you, too,' I said to Çiğdem, and you should have seen the expression on her face. This time she didn't just grin. Turning to face me, she looked me in the eye and jabbed me with her gaze, 'Well, what're you waiting for? Aren't you a man? Defend me!' I wasn't expecting this, to tell the truth. Uncertain what to say, I sat motionless, like cut stone. Then, softly, she said, 'Never mind; he's not worth fighting.' My little lover, my rough woman! What is she doing now, I wonder? Who is she with? Who are her friends? Perhaps she, too, had left for Europe and never returned to Istanbul. As I reflect on it now, I think Çiğdem's perpetually bottled-up anger or her obsession with speed – that turned into what the headlines nowadays call 'road rage' – had as much to do with the martial law as with her repressed femininity. And her incarcerated brother. So many young lives squandered, a scorched landscape still barren… the remains of the past. True, some of us were spared, but those who were hurt were hurt badly.

In the days following the generals' memorandum, I remember a sergeant trying to guide traffic on Taksim Square, wielding a handgun, shouting after the cars. For some reason, he threatened to 'burn' rather than 'roast' the errant drivers. Just for ignoring him and taking the roundabout carelessly, the sergeant would burn us. We too, due to our speed, were in danger of smoking an innocent bystander. In reality, our goal was neither to be burned or roasted nor to smoke anyone. Our bodies loose with alcohol, we were searching for pleasure. Speed was among the requisites of this search. I remember driving at full speed on those tree-lined boulevards – not too many in the Istanbul of those years – or diving into the narrow streets without slowing down. Çiğdem always managed to take the curves at the last second, without shifting gears, and just when I could feel my heart lurching to my throat. Other things would come up my throat, too. Certainly not the words, 'Slow down!' Pale and panic-stricken, I'd still want to shout, 'Faster! Faster! Floor it!' Then my mouth would dry up, my tongue would stick to the roof of my mouth. That's when Çiğdem's right hand would let go of the steering wheel, and come to rest on my trouser buttons. She would undo them one by one while passing the slow cars. How she managed to do that, I still don't know. I said it before, her hands had a God-given talent. They were both beautiful, very beautiful, and nimble. I would feel her fingers on my manhood as it hardened. The faster she drove, the faster her hand moved. My moans would mix with the engine noise of the Anadol and its bodywork that we liked to mock. But the engine was sturdy, and the faster the crankshaft revolved, the more tightly the cylinder clutched the rings and oiled pistons! We would drive through deserted streets, along dark stone houses that let no light through their drawn curtains. My legs would tense with pleasure that surged through my thighs. Çiğdem would check the road from time to time, but mostly she would watch me, my widening pupils, my twisted lips. I myself couldn't recognize my face in the rearview mirror. She would max the radio volume. Not so that she could keep her right hand's tempo as it moved faster and faster to the rhythms of The Beatles, but to muffle my screams while I neared orgasm.

For the longest time, I thought that, more than me or the pleasure she gave me, Çiğdem loved the exhilaration of tempting death at peak speeds. I still think so. Otherwise, our lovemaking would have been different. She would have let me inside her at least once. I wonder if she was a virgin? If so, I hope she remained a virgin and never replaced her car. Avenues emptying right before the curfew hour, our frenzied descent to the sea, the screech of car brakes in the rain, the red, yellow, green traffic lights reflecting off the wet pavement… Maybe these images were what drove us to pessimism, spurring our desire to 'die fighting' – in the revolutionary lingo of those years. Thankfully, we didn't die fighting. As much as I enjoyed chewing her name, I never attempted to eat Çiğdem (unlike the Japanese student), and she always took the curve at the last moment, while using her right hand and left hand simultaneously and with equal skill. We never saw each other after we broke up. I don't know whether she had, but I had other lovers since then. I was even in a car accident with one, although I still have not owned a car. As for the meaning of her name, Çiğdem, I looked it up recently, while writing this story. It means 'crocus' or 'drowsy blossom,' in the vernacular.

Translated by Aron R. Aji

A Couple of People

Sema Kaygusuz

FROM THE MOMENT I first heard his horrible moaning dominating the night, I was both repulsed by how close the suffering was, and reluctant to seek out the source. And yet between stepping out of my door and walking down the stairs, its sorrowful resonance began to seem less convincing. The voice had been coming right through my bedroom wall, creeping into all the rooms of my home, reverberating in my ears. And although I'm prone to suffering from pain myself, I was cynical enough to recognize an artificial dimension to this familiar sound. This moaning brought to mind someone using every means possible to make himself cry. No tears, but a considerable amount of sobbing.

It is not easy to describe pain. It makes you stutter unwillingly. Leaving aside the silvery shimmering of pain, people who make themselves important through their suffering nauseate me. I am scared of someone who immediately begins to talk about his suffering before giving one a chance to read his soul through the lines on his face. As if I were deemed responsible for binding his wounds.

Inner pain is a noble feeling. It does not turn you into a fool like joy can. Taking its force from unknown darkness, even hurling the body to the depths, it turns a human being into a marvelous geometrical shape, perfect as a globe made of one single pain. It does not unnerve you with screams and sobs, crying as if it were the end of life! It does not consume your patience with its night-long moaning! It just remains silent and throbs. When it remains silent, the world becomes deaf. Behind the flames of fiery thoughts as they burn to embers and turn to pure light, there shines a sincere wisdom. Someone suffering real pain, who accepts that he can never fully grasp the concrete meaning of anything, aches quietly under the curse of feeling everything in life to the marrow.

That is why, on one of those nights when I was nearly crazed from lack of sleep, I hesitated to go to him on hearing his bitter moans. His wailing was so spoiled, so impertinent. It started first with a pitiful whine, and after nobody came, the pitch was increasingly ill-tempered, reaching a peak at high C, after which he would abruptly fall silent for a moment, take a deep breath, rest and then return to the annoying beginning. I hung around the stairs for a minute, seeking the source of the noise. I listened at all the doors one by one. Most probably it was coming from the building next door. When I left the house, I stood on the hill at the top of Inonu Avenue that descends to Gümüşsuyu.

At night, this place becomes a land of cats. The cats sleeping on the pavement jumped up in fear and looked at my face nervously. I always find it unsettling how cats know to look at the eyes in order to read trouble. This is more knowledge than an animal can carry! But I suppose, they are urban cats. This must be why, in Istanbul, almost everybody's ancestors come from somewhere else, but the ancestors of the cats, dogs, doves and seagulls settled in this city long ago. This must be the place where they gathered their knowledge of humans.

The cats dispersed quickly as I stepped among them. Feeling, as usual, that I had no space of my own, I let myself go down rapidly towards the sea. I moved so fast I could feel the pain in my heels go all the way to my chest. At the same time, I could still hear that sound of heart-breaking, painful moaning. The vibrations penetrated me despite the siren of the freight boat passing through the strait and the screaming of seagulls. It kept pushing me downward, toward the ships.

The air was filled with the smell of diesel fuel from the boats approaching the Karaköy pier. At daybreak the lights on the opposite shore had already started to fade. I walked to the waterside park next to the university and sat down on my usual bench. Once I met someone on that bench. He had pointed to some seagulls perched in a row on the breakwater and said they resembled ancient Roman senators with togas on their shoulders, but as I am always very shy with strangers, I didn't even raise my head to glance at him. In the essence of meeting someone new, there is always an unforeseen life, intrinsic to this specific encounter. The mysterious unknown in the question, 'What if we had never met?' exists in the very nature of such a meeting. And then, all that is experienced becomes just a shiver of the thought of what can never be lived. I have always tended toward that which is never going to be lived, and left it at that.

It took place on a suffocating summer day. A Sunday… The smell of grilled meat was wafting in the air as families gathered under the laurels in the park and laughter rose from men drinking beer in the cars parked by the sea. Istanbul people love the streets. When the weather is nice, a flood of people descend to the shores of the Bosphorus as if they had some old account to settle with the city. They turn the area into a fairground, with their fishing lines, picnic baskets and baby buggies. Seeming to play out old memories of distant homelands by flowing waters, they stretch out wherever they find the smallest patches of grass, or flowers, or in the verdant areas around the ancient city walls. This is why the Istanbul landscape is actually just an allusion to somewhere else. The joyful mourning of what has been lost is being performed with this site as a backdrop. Those who experience the real city are those who dare to see the city without any allusions. A couple of people who can control their sorrow, who unlike others don't rely on the eclectic architectural beauty of the Dolmabahçe Palace to cover the sewage smell spreading in fine waves from Dolmabahçe. A noisy, crowded city consisting of the solitude of a couple of people... While I was about to melt out of solitude in the midst of all those noises, he came and sat beside me. As I said, I am not a very talkative person. Besides, I couldn't care less what the seagulls on the breakwater looked like. I pulled my book out of my bag and started reading, while he kept cracking and eating sunflower seeds. Now and then, when I turned a page, I raised my head, glanced at the Bosphorus and dove back into my book. The man had lost all interest in me. Then, a younger man approached on a noisy motorcycle and parked his vehicle right in front of us. Unluckily for us, on top of that he had a sound system installed. He disembarked, removed his helmet and started playing some awful music. Now I could neither see the sea, nor understand what I was reading with all this noise.

'Look at him, how inconsiderate!' I snapped, loud enough for my neighbour on the bank to hear.

'Don't get cross,' he said, cracking his sunflower seeds. 'He is making his mark on time.'

Early in the morning, sitting on the bench and recalling that marked point in time, I was startled by the pitiful tone of the voice nagging at me again. Once more, right in my ear, so obvious to anyone listening, a human being in decline. Suddenly I lost my temper. In the morning chill, I felt as though I were in a film, a melancholy figure in a historical tragedy, painting the loneliness of a couple of people onto the mood of the entire city of Istanbul, while the other character was suffering behind walls that belong to no city on Earth. There's no more cowardly form of existence than holding onto learned suffering. I stood up hastily. The crisp March air revived me. A vital cold licked at my face. Something that belonged to this world... Life is dreadful, I concluded. Yet, sometimes, life can indeed be fine.

When I stepped out to the street from Kabataş Park, I found myself in the midst of a hellish traffic jam. I noticed the vanity of the bank clerks in dark suits as they passed by their reflections in the glass doors, and this relieved me. Just a normal day. No need to exaggerate things. I found myself straining a little as I climbed the steep slope back to Gümüşsuyu from Kabataş, passing among high school boys with voices only just broken, making remarks which normally shouldn't be said aloud in public. As the estate agent was rolling up the shutters of his shop, he smiled at me as if anticipating a boring chat. I could sense the time passing minute-by-minute, just by looking at people's faces. That was when I realized I was no longer hearing that pathetic moaning. I guess it escaped my notice when I became distracted. Like the pulse. Only when it penetrated under my skin was I able to feel it. Otherwise it was like sour notes fading in the distance among the street noises. But as I approached home, I started to hear those pitiful sounds. Life was ringing in my ears again...

As I entered the door, I was taken by surprise. The voice had conquered the entire building. It was echoing down the stairwell, shaking the railings, almost materialised enough to be grasped in hand, even distinguishable as a warm existence. It licked my face with its wet tongue. In need of attention... sociable...intimidating as a beggar. Leaning to the walls for support, I climbed to my flat on the third floor. It was stuffy inside. My things were all over the floor. The television had been left on, pages ripped from books strewn about, dirty laundry lying everywhere, the house totally stinking.

When I entered my bedroom, I found him staring at the ceiling with bloodshot eyes. His mouth was stretched open, his body distorted from the constant moaning.

'Shut up!' I screamed. 'Shut up! Shut up! Whatever it is you're feeling, you can't make me feel the essence of it. The deeper the pain lies, the more difficult it is to speak of. Impossible in fact. That's why I can't talk to you either. I can't translate myself into your Turkish. Instead of quietly enduring my own waves of pain that no one else understands, instead of breaking my silence by telling my sufferings just to convince you that I am suffering too, I'll simply stitch your hungry, brassy mouth with a quilt needle!'

Then, I lay down beside him. We two, just a couple of people crowded in together as if a multitude of thousands, slept the sleep of millions.

Translated by Carol Yürür

The Well

Türker Armaner

THEY VISITED AGAIN last night, late last night. I wasn't yet asleep; actually I never go to sleep easily. The time when I used to have long, deep sleeps now seems consigned to history.

I didn't get out of bed, but just waited for them to go. My hand reached for the handle of the pistol that I always kept loaded and ready by my side. They didn't come into my bedroom at all. If I ever see one of them in the doorway, I'll put the pistol to my temple and pull the trigger.

They wandered around the living room without even putting the lights on. I listened to their footsteps pass in front of my window and move away. I had no idea how many of them there were, but there was more than one.

I switched on the bedside lamp and put on my glasses, which had been lying next to it. Everything now looked clearer.

A dog ran down the street and startled me. It was all too much for my tired old body. I got up and took a cardigan from the pile of clothes heaped in the armchair and put it around my shoulders. I lit a cigarette and began reading my half-finished book.

I woke up to the atonal, metallic sound of the muezzin's voice[1]. It was getting light. Of course I was unable to see the sky, but the street was clearly visible. I raised my hand to my eyes and my fingers touched the lens

---

1. muezzin – Mosque official who calls people to prayer five times a day from the minaret.

19

of my glasses. The book had fallen to the floor; the ash of my cigarette had lengthened and some of it had dropped onto the bed. *One day I'll cause an accident*, I told myself. *People are probably right not to want lonely old people as neighbours.*

I left the cigarette in the ashtray, removed my glasses and, curling up under the quilt, tried to sleep a bit more.

When I woke again, the church bells were ringing and I realised it was time to get up. I dressed, popped a few biscuits into my mouth from the packet lying in the kitchen, picked up my book and left the house. I climbed the stairs and hesitated for a moment when I reached the street door, just as I did every day. They could be waiting for me at the corner of the street, on the pavement, in the local shop, anywhere.

A neighbour on his way to work greeted me with a nod and opened the door; I launched myself outside.

It was almost noon. I'd been drinking coffee and reading the newspaper in the café on the seafront for about three and a half hours. For years, I'd spent my mornings going over the preceding night in my mind. Why did they postpone my interrogation? What were they looking for in my tiny basement?

My sole aim in life now was to keep my hand on the trigger and kill myself before falling into their hands, because I no longer had the strength to retaliate. I could have done once, years ago when I was young and strong, when I slept long and deep.

Was it really sleep that was bringing them to me? Were these people, who I thought I had pushed to the back of my mind but who now managed to get into my living room, the inevitable imaginings of an old man's sleep?

I thought I was losing my marbles; I'd probably long been seen as a senile old man. However, if I had really been persuaded of that, I would have assumed they were merely the product of a sick mind and I'd have stopped trying to escape.

Could I stop?

Can a person let go of fear once he knows that he himself is the root of his fear?

Is it possible to know these things?

If only I could have finished my book.

I lit a cigarette.

How could it be me creating such tangible manifestations? In the darkest hours of night – despite two locks and a bolt – the sound they made as they forced open the door, the inauspicious, rhythmic clatter as they wandered about on the parquet floor, the changing reflections made by their darting torches, the bolts I found unlocked in the morning…

It couldn't be me creating all that; especially knowing that they believed they had valid reasons for coming after me.

I couldn't talk to anyone about it, nor could I write about it. Someone who is being stalked should never do anything so imprudent.

Perhaps I should have put an end to those years of torture, without waiting for them to come into my room. But I was curious. I wanted to know who had held such a grudge against me for forty-two years, and how that person intended to settle it.

I decided to go down to Kadıköy[2]. I paid my bill and left, turning off the main road into some side streets. I was unable to stay in a big space or crowded street for long. Increasingly, the sounds of people and cars made me feel as if I was suffocating, descending to the bottom of a rapid

2. Kadıköy – A large and populous district, on the Asian side of the Bosphorus.

whirlpool.

A lonely street is always safer. You notice each new thing and are ready for any danger. Evil shapes emerge onto the stage of an empty street one by one, making your brain, muscles, nerves, and veins tense up.

Crowds constitute a threat in themselves; they're intrinsically bad.

Passing the road that runs perpendicular to my street, I came out in front of the Greek school. Then I turned left and walked towards the sea. The pavement was now crowded; I paused a while, gazing at the sea and the historic peninsula, like a blind man.

If, when I was weaving my destiny, two eagles had snatched the threads I'd put in place and taken them somewhere else, would everything have turned out very different?

I think I was right to choose an underground place when preparing my end. A person's death should take place where his conscious self feels at home.

For a long time, I had lived in various neighbourhoods on the other side of the Bosphorus. Nobody, not even my lovers, ever knew my address. I would always go to their places, or we'd spend time together at guest houses. Hotels were dangerous because, to book a room, I had to fill in a form and show my identity card.

During the time I was getting by on translation work, I didn't have a bank account for my royalties; in any case, I would use a different pseudonym for every article, every book.

I don't remember all the houses I've lived in. That's not because my memory is failing with age; quite the opposite, I remember everything very well – including those days when I entered the faculty, sixty-seven years ago, and finished in first place sixty-three years ago. I was always in hiding; because I kept running away, my brain developed a reflex of its own accord: it would hide my past from myself.

After a while, the hunter and the hunted unite under the concept of 'hunt'. Apart from the need to pass regular reports to his superior, the first forgets why he is doing it and the second forgets why he is running away.

It was months since I had been across to Istanbul. Perhaps I could never go back now. When I lived on that side, Kadıköy was a refuge where I could disappear. I would be the last passenger to board the ferry; thus, the hunter would be behind the very last one and get left on the quayside. I would try not to do it too often so that they wouldn't stalk me on this side as well.

As I jumped off the ferry, I would sense being inside those walls that fell six centuries ago. The walls that Valens stole from Kadıköy would immediately weave my fear into the fabric of the quayside area.

Where was that Aqueduct of Valens, I wonder?

I screwed up my eyes like a blind man. I could no longer see my past or my future. The city walls were no longer there. If escape requires a shelter, your only recourse is a dark, bottomless well.

I crossed the road and, diving once again into the side streets, headed up towards Muvakkıthane Caddesi to browse among the second-hand books. As I was looking at the stalls lining the cobbled street, a woman in her forties asked me in perfect English for some money.

I'd seen this woman two years ago in Beyoğlu[3]. It hadn't seemed strange to see a homeless Englishwoman there, but it surprised me to see her in Kadıköy, and it frightened me a little.

---

3. Beyoğlu – A famous district known for its café culture and nightlife, situated on the European side of the Bosphorus.

I looked at the woman's pale skin and blue eyes. She was wearing a red headscarf and a shabby multi-coloured dress. Was she here because she had run away? Or had they expanded surveillance to international levels?

Without taking my eyes off hers, I took some money from my waistcoat pocket and gave it to her. She thanked me and went away. I felt my pulse; it was racing. I looked to see where she went, but she had disappeared. The streetlights were very bright, and the conversations of people passing on either side of me sounded distant. I saw a gypsy playing an accordion on the street corner. The sound of his music was now all I could hear. He was playing a waltz. Next to him, the head-scarved woman was collecting money. I'd danced to this music with a blonde, blue-eyed woman in the capital city of an Eastern European country forty-three years ago. The street started to turn in time to the music. I wanted to light a cigarette, but couldn't find the packet. My book fell out of my hand. A bearded, bespectacled youth sitting on a wicker stool in front of a second-hand bookshop rose and walked towards me.

I was now sitting on the stool where the youth had sat.

'You were about to faint,' he said. 'Please, have some water.'

I'd fallen right into their arms now. I had shown just how unwise it was to go out into a crowded street.

'Thank you, son. If you don't mind, I'll just smoke a cigarette. I won't take up any more of your time.'

I looked for my cigarette packet and found it quickly this time. The cigarette brought me to my senses. A dark girl with long wavy hair was with the youth. 'I hope you're feeling better,' she said. 'Would you like me to call a doctor?'

'No, no thank you,' I said. I think my voice was a bit loud. Fear that cannot be managed renders a person even weaker.

24

I adjusted my tone of voice. 'I just felt a bit dizzy,' I said. 'It'll pass in a moment.'

'Do you teach German philology?' asked the youth.

'No. Why?'

'You're reading Machiavelli in German.'

'It's a book on Machiavelli by a German philosopher.'

The book I'd dropped was lying on the table. The youth had confused the title with the author's name, if this wasn't all a game, that is, of course…

He looked at the book again, and appeared somewhat disconcerted.

'You've got Machiavelli, haven't you?' the girl asked the youth and, without waiting for a reply, reached out towards the shelves. As she removed the book, I read the name on the back of the book.

'That's a book by Gramsci,' I said, 'It was written in honour of Machiavelli. I think the book you were talking about is on the top shelf.'

The youth got up, found the book and took it down. He looked pleased.

'Yes, this is it,' he said, 'I'd like to give it to you.'

'Thank you,' I said, 'I read it years ago in Italian.'

I was beginning to let my guard down in the face of this courtesy. I needed to go before I became too distracted.

They offered me tea, but I refused. They were probably thinking what a rude old man I was. It was a long time since I'd accepted a drink from anyone, except at the tea garden I went to every day. My throat burns and I am unable to swallow whenever someone offers me a glass of anything, even if I don't drink it.

'We're in our second year at law school,' said the youth.

My head began to spin again.

'I've seen you reading and making notes in the tea garden on the seafront at Moda[4]. I'd wanted to speak to you

---

4. Moda – A gentrified area on the Asian side of the Bosphorus.

but never had the courage. Can you recommend some reading material in this field?'

It was time to leave, without showing any anxiety. Saying I would be back, I rose, thanked them for their concern and left; I was able to leave. Could the fact that I was not harmed be construed as evidence that they were not among the hunters?

I spent fifteen minutes sitting on one of the benches facing the quayside. Clearly, I hadn't managed to erase myself from everything, even though I'd spoken to hardly anyone in that neighbourhood.

After a lifetime of fleeing, I assume everyone is a hunter and find traces of my past in their faces. In the Englishwoman, I saw my lover of half a century ago; in the youth I saw my university years.

I watched ferries and motorboats approaching and leaving the jetty, people boarding and disembarking, newspaper vendors, people queuing to use telephones, the darkening sea, the shoeshine boys, and barefoot gypsy girls selling flowers.

None of the people I watched was aware that I was looking at them. And I was not aware that I was being watched; in fact I thought that no-one was looking at me. They say that talking to the young keeps old people young. I mustn't fall into that trap.

I reflected that the feeling of defeat that envelops me when darkness falls had also permeated the area; yet there was no hint of anger against the victor. Kadıköy was resigned to defeat, and resignation never speaks.

I went up to Moda in a dolmuş[5]. As a precaution, I didn't alight outside my house, but one street before, and walked.

---

5. dolmuş – A taxi with a semi-fixed route around the city.

THE WELL

As I opened the front door, the emptiness of the apartment building and the twisting staircase down to the basement reminded me of that time before sleep. Every night when I get into bed, I see a black emptiness descend over everything. I pressed the timed light switch and went down the stairs and into my apartment. Immediately, I locked and bolted the door.

I took out some pasta left over from the previous day, put it on the picnic gas stove and started stirring it with a wooden spoon. My glasses steamed up and I wiped them on my shirtsleeve. When the sputtering increased, I turned off the gas and took the pan into the living room and, shoving away the pile of papers on the table with my elbow, put it on a mat.

As I ate, I thought about what I had to do that evening. I had to classify the subtitles and references in the dossier. Every time I read it, a number of amendments needed to be made, though that number was gradually decreasing. I would read through the whole thing once more and put my references inside parentheses and into the bibliography. It would be good if I could finish the text that evening. I would try to feed my notes into the beginning of the sixth section. I wanted to submit it to the publishers now. After the thousands of books and articles I had read, this was the only original work I would publish.

It would come out under a different name, but that didn't matter to me at all. For me, the main thing was the action of writing itself. Throughout my long life, I'd been saying that 'thinking' was meaningless on its own. Ideas appear to form in the thinker's head, but the text produced by those ideas is rooted in other texts and analyses of those texts.

The only thing I was bothered about was language. I had read most of the books that were useful to me in the original language, but this book I'd written in my own language. My publisher said the language needed to be 'simplified'. I had no idea how my book would turn out as a result of that. I had insisted on seeing it after 'simplification' and before publication, which he accepted. But did I have enough time?

It was a good thing I'd typed it all out.

I took the washing-up into the kitchen and left it in the sink. I needed to work now.

I attached a reed to my pencil stub and sharpened the lead, then attached another reed to a red pencil. I started by writing the title 'A Critique of Nineteenth Century German State Idealism' in red, and then, systematically, wrote up my final notes.

It was almost half past one. I had been working continuously for about five hours. I was tired. I glanced towards my bedroom. As my sleep grew heavier, the well was becoming narrower and the darkness at its mouth was spreading. I checked the locks and bolt, emptied the ashtrays, turned out the lights and went to bed.

A dirty bar, with a cracked plaster ceiling. As my breathing deepened, the ceiling rose upwards, and the bed dropped downwards. With each breath, the light entering through the narrow windows dimmed; darkness enveloped me and I felt like a mummy wrapped in strips of bandage. I wanted to open my arms and escape those bonds, but the strips came up to my throat, to my face. With difficulty, I passed the fingers of my right hand along the barrel of my pistol. The cold of its steel spread throughout my body and made me feel safe.

I fell asleep.

When I felt the torchlight on my face, I immediately

searched for the pistol. It was in the palm of my hand. I couldn't keep my eyes open because of the blinding whiteness. I cocked the pistol with my thumb. The light was directed at my face for a few seconds; I couldn't see who it was, but I heard the sound of footsteps going into the living room. 'He's in the bedroom,' said a woman's voice. 'He's asleep.'

There were three people in there, two men and a woman. I heard them whispering, but couldn't make out what they said. A barely visible light was filtering into my room. I heard a rustling of papers. Perhaps they were rifling through my dossier. I threw off the quilt and, holding the pistol, got up. I moved towards the door. Hearing the sound of the typewriter, I stopped; they were writing something. Their whisperings blended with the sound of the typewriter. They were in the dark, shining the torch on it.

I wanted to take another step forwards, but bumped into the armchair. 'It's all over now,' I thought.
The sounds stopped.

I entered the living room and put on the light. Nobody was there. My dossier was in a complete mess. I saw a piece of paper stuck in the typewriter. I looked at the door and froze. The locks and bolt were in place, and the windows were closed. Yet they had been in the apartment.

I turned on all the lights and looked everywhere, in the far corners of each room, in the kitchen, bathroom, wardrobe and library.

Nobody.

It was impossible for me to sleep. I put a pillow behind my back, sat on the bed, and waited with the pistol in my hand.

I woke up cold. It was almost six o'clock. I got up and dressed. It occurred to me to look at the piece of paper stuck in the typewriter. Fearfully, I tried to read it without touching it. On it was written a date and place, no more: 21.8.1940 / Mexico City.

I let myself out. At that hour, I didn't expect anyone to open the door for me. I buttoned up my raincoat and started walking. It was the first time they had sent me such a clear signal.

It was going to be a long day.

I walked from Moda Caddesi to Bahariye, and from there down to Altıyol. I hadn't been down that road for a long time. The shops were not yet open. After a while, the sound of successive shutters being raised would indicate that Bahariye was ready for customers.

My steps took me to Yeldeğirmen[6]. I had nothing to do there, nobody to see; it was just where I went.

I used to feel comfortable in that neighbourhood; for me, it was a place of exile, for people like me. I knew all about exile from my time living in Ayaspaşa, Tarlabaşı and Tepebaşı. This was my place of exile in Kadıköy, though I had never lived there.

I started to wander through the narrow streets. Washing was drying on lines hung between opposite buildings. Sheets, stockings, underwear, shirts, black primary school aprons were hanging side by side, as if protecting the banished soul of the neighbourhood. The walls of the houses where washing was hanging were damp and cold; their entrances smelled of mildew. Rubbish had piled up outside the doors of deserted buildings.

I felt safe there.

I had grown used to police surveillance, but the running away had started later, after I was interrogated by my friends. I hadn't supported the regime, but I'd supported the exile

6. Yeldeğirmen – A district of Kadıköy.

on Büyükada[7], for both social and aesthetic reasons. It was when I discovered the contradictions that I'd started making systematic notes for my book. In theory, I was ahead of everyone else because I'd decided to learn another language in order to read the texts in the original.

I ordered Russian grammar books and a dictionary from abroad, and my lover and I started trying to learn the language together. As expected, she got bored and gave up. After months of effort, I attained the level at which I could read the texts. During that time, I lost my lover.

She was among my interrogators.

There was a knock at the door of my house in Ayaspaşa late one night; I was working. I thought it was the Political Branch, so I locked my notes away in the desk drawer. The next time, they banged loudly on the door. Before opening it, I asked who it was. When I heard their voices, I relaxed.

My former lover entered with two friends.

'We need to speak,' they said.

It was after hearing those words that the mouth of the well started to open up for me. I see that now, as I've come closer to the bottom of the well over the last few days.

When they left, it was getting light. I lit a cigarette and thought about what had happened. They had asked me to give up my ideas, but they really meant the person they thought I supported. I wasn't supporting anyone. I had analysed the texts, but the conclusion contradicted the reality in my head. I had established that reality from what I had read. There were no texts to support the other side. They were definitely defending a particular person.

How do you defend a person? In my view, there are two ways: text and action. Unless you are witnessed – which

---

7. Büyükada– The largest of the 'Princes Islands' in the Sea of Marmara, near Istanbul.

is not always possible – the second of those also counts as text.

Perhaps that is what I was really being accused of, the fact that I saw everything as text. They used to say I always stayed on the shore, on the edge. Yet to reach the shore you have to cross a piece of land or set off along a path. I never had a piece of land that belonged to me, nor a shore to stand on.

It was evening. I could have written those words in the first light of morning or the noon sunshine. I didn't feel as if I'd reached the end of a linear path or completed a circle. Nothing had changed; darkness had fallen over my own time. I realised it wasn't my duty to make reality conform to what people said.

However, the day was now really coming to an end. The well would soon draw me inside.

They arrived. The door wasn't forced. I was waiting, unblinking, with the pistol loaded and the lamp turned on. I had my dossier next to me. That book would be the only indication that I had existed. They had left a note the previous night. They wanted to tell me that the writer of the dossier they had rifled through would come to the same end as the writer of the texts I had read. As far as I was concerned, there was no need for the written word to be reality or for reality to be the written word.

I knew the light of the torch was passing over my desk. They were looking for what I had written. They talked among themselves, and I heard two of them go out. They didn't close the door when they left. Cold was coming in and I began to shiver. I got to my feet. The increasing cold was breaking my resolve, but I wasn't afraid of coming face to face with them. I aimed the barrel, not at my temples but at the doorway of my bedroom. Everything had ceased to exist apart from my breath and the sound of footsteps.

The sound of footsteps grew louder; a shadow fell across the furnishings in my room. The shadow lengthened, to my wardrobe, and from there it climbed on to my bed.

I squeezed the trigger. Seeing a figure enter, I'd aimed the barrel at where I thought it should be; I wasn't going to let anyone interrogate me. The smell of gunpowder and blood reached my nose. I reeled and fired one shot after another. As the bullet wound opened up in my body, the door to the street closed. I was no longer cold. I was sliding downwards, down the damp walls of the well.

I looked up and saw it watching me at the mouth of the well.

Translated by Ruth Whitehouse

A Question

Müge İplikçi

A BENCH BETWEEN two decorative pools. Three elderly women are sitting on the bench. One dressed in purple, one blonde. One's name begins with the letter N. One's name ends with K. The snow-white hair of the third means she is remembered in conjunction with someone called Kenan. When the three women are together, their ages total 195. Almost two centuries. Easy to say! Moreover, it's not only their ages, but also their feelings that span two centuries. The age of the one whose name ends in K is ten years less than N's, and the snow-white haired one's age is ten years more. Together, they turn on the taps to the pools, and then forget to turn them off.

At that point, Şehnaz was stuck.

She had just worked out the three women's ages: one was 75, another was 65 and the last was 55. Even their names were clear in her head: Nur Hanım, Dilek Hanım and Sisifus Hanım. That's when she formulated the love between Sisifus Hanım and Kenan Bey. But the question was not about the ages of those women. It was not a problem about ages, nor a logical question about the problems of age. It was an equation concerning pools. But it wasn't exactly a question about pools. Şehnaz was convinced that the women sitting on the bench between two decorative pools who had forgotten to turn off the taps were looking at her. She shivered. Soon, the shivering would turn to despair. Because the question was not how many hours it would take to fill the pools, or how long before they overflowed.

Şehnaz was confused.

Raising her head from the booklet in front of her, she

tried to make out the classroom where she was sitting, to catch the scent of early summer trying to enter through the classroom window, to pick out the sharp colours of the Bosphorus.

It was 1984, and Şehnaz was in a musty classroom taking the Student Selection and Placement Centre, or SSPC, annual 2nd stage examination. On the green board, someone had written 9:30-12:30 with broken chalk. Smudged by traces of lime, those rounded figures provided a hint of the writer's character. It was the writing of condemned hands: the writing of hands trapped between a destiny of chance appointment or being moved around like a piece in a game of checkers.

Who owned those hands? Young teachers dressed in shot-silk Indian skirts standing at the front near the examiner's desk. Every so often they would look at the watches with leather straps around their delicate wrists, at the door to the corridor, at the draughty expanse of corridor, then back at a different point inside; their gazes escaped to the view of the Bosphorus that Şehnaz had just been looking at. They were escapist teachers; escapists, sweet young idealists, romantics.

If Şehnaz had not wanted to be a doctor, she could have been one of those strange romantics who had outlived themselves. Her biology teacher always said to her: after you finish university, you could stay on at college; you could be a doctor and teach at the same time...

Şehnaz had seen the sense in this; she prepared herself to sit the university examination accordingly. The saying 'don't count your chickens before they hatch' was just a collection of words for her that were old, out of date, their meaning lost. She told herself that people determine their own destiny; they can do whatever they want to do.

According to her biology teacher, and her own plans for gaining a place at medical school, there had really only been one question remaining on the road towards the old question of logic and pools. That one question was the obstacle. Until that question, Şehnaz had found a solution to every question that confronted her. But faced with that question, she felt completely helpless, because it was not a question of logic – about three women sitting between two decorative pools – but an illogical, unhinged, senseless question.

It should have been about Nur Hanım, Sisifus Hanım and Dilek Hanım sitting at that magnificent Bosphorus viewpoint, presided over by the Halide Edip Adıvar Lycee in Beylerbeyi, one of the select neighbourhoods on the Bosphorus. In that case, the question Şehnaz would have asked herself would have been:

What happens next?

What happens next? Şehnaz had never counted on this. She hadn't believed that the headscarf she would remove when entering college and replace when leaving college could stand between her and enrolment at medical school, getting on with being a university student, and staying on at college to teach. Furthermore, there were the promises her future held for her, and the way she would handle those promises…

What happens next? It would be a question Şehnaz would ask herself frequently after that. And she would be unable to find words to explain it. Because the worst memories, like the best moments in life, cannot be explained.

Şehnaz was to hold on at college for seven years. She would pass through seven doors of life, giving up a piece of herself at each of them. First her headscarf, then an invisible fracture due to insults, then another invisible fracture due to denial, then another invisible fracture due to contempt, then another invisible fracture due to being forced to exist, then another invisible fracture due to being counted as nothing… In the end, she would leave college behind her like some forgotten item on a bench.

What happens next?

What happens when a person is considered totally worthless?

There will be references to Şehnaz in theses, articles and footnotes about the headscarf issue, yet she will be unable to write her own thesis, article or footnotes.

What happens next? Don't count your chickens before they hatch. Şehnaz with the diploma will become a housewife. She will make wishes and yearn to be bathed in celestial light, but her destiny will remain like that of Sisifus.

In that musty classroom in 1984, Şehnaz looked at the invigilators whose faces shimmered in the myriad of Bosphorus colours filtering through the window. There, for the first time, she understood that clues to the future are hidden in the present, and that the present has the power to dictate the future with a question, a colour, or a smell. She felt that, for some unknown reason, on the day she dropped out of university, she would run to Beylerbeyi and sit alone on a bench, pondering her differences and similarities, feeling the deep blue of the Bosphorus with its carousel of colours burning her eyes. Looking around her, she would realise she was in the garden of Beylerbeyi Palace, sitting on the bench between two decorative pools.

'We see the future, but what's the point?'

That is the question she would probably be asking.

However, Şehnaz is now very forgetful. She feels old and tired. Like so many women who shelve the question of what happens next, she slowly makes her way out of Beylerbeyi Palace – the last visitor of the day.

Translated by Ruth Whitehouse

Out of Reach

Gönül Kıvılcım

Hand

NİLÜFER HAD A close bond with the many corners of the island and a special affection for its cats and bougainvillea and wild gardens. But there was nothing to beat going down Panjur Street to the quay, to rendezvous with the water there. Panjur Street was a picture with its tabby cats, its empty demijohns, its Algida ice cream umbrellas and the brooms for sale at the grocer's. All the way from America came Haluk Bey, to complete the picture.

Ever since the young son of the house arrived home, Nilüfer's daily life had become a trivial detail alongside the feelings that pierced a hole in her stomach. The ugly tablecloth bought in Egypt, the chats by the swimming pool sprinkled throughout with pearls of contempt.

Nilüfer sat down on the stone steps in Panjur Street. Silence all around. Except for the perpetual motion of the pump for the pool of the neighbouring villa. Just that. Never in her life had she suffered such pain. She envied the daylight that slipped through the shutters and stole into Haluk Bey's room, the light free to touch his eyes drowsy with sleep, to envelop his body in its warm embrace, and to love Haluk Bey completely, not just bit by bit.

Really, she was used to the fact that anything her hand reached for was unattainable. She had spent all her life under the sheltering roof of others. At the age of twelve she fetched and carried for a man who had made a name for himself as a sculptor; at fourteen she changed nappies for a spoiled baby; at sixteen she cleaned up the crap for a bad-tempered 'madam' (and so bad-tempered!) and for the remaining ten years had worked as general domestic in Mistress Billur Hanım's joyless household.

And still, the unbearable knowledge that three months later, at the end of summer, she would never see Haluk Bey again, strengthened her attraction to the family's son who studied in America. Like the sudden collapse of the pine tree that had remained upright for years, Haluk Bey too would be lost and gone. When that time came, Nilüfer had no idea how she would preserve the feeling that had leapt from the hand of the young son of the house into hers and was like stomach-ache or a fit of delirium.

It all began the day the old pine tree gave itself up to the earth.

As though it had heard Nilüfer's love-moans, the creaky hundred-year-old tree, rotten at the core, had toppled over and blocked the steps that led down to the summer house. Now what? The thought that she would not see Haluk Bey again until the tree was removed made her envy it with its dead branches. She wanted to stretch lifeless beside it.

Standing by the tree, deep in thought, behind the garden gate that joined the white-shuttered house to the road, Nilüfer jumped.

'What happened here?' It was Haluk Bey.

'Don't ask,' said Nilüfer. 'The huge pine tree picked on us and just keeled over.' They stood by the tree. That day, by a stroke of luck, the young man of the house who for weeks had never stirred from his seat, happened to have gone running with a pack of morning joggers. Now he and Nilüfer sat on the steps at the entrance with all that was left of the tree – its roots.

'I'm ravenous,' Haluk Bey muttered. Nilüfer showed him the eggs in her plastic bag.

'I was going to make you fried eggs.'

'I can't go down to the shops in this sweaty state. They'll be worried about me at home, don't you think?'

They were under the bougainvillea that spread and clung to the garden wall. Haluk's lips opened and closed. She had a good look at his face, his long body, his lips plump as an almond, his eyes thoughtful as though planning a chess move, and the lock of hair, brown as a hazelnut shell, that fell over his forehead.

She was in no state to listen, but asked him about America, if only to make him say something, so she could see those almond lips opening and closing.

Desire was slowly rising in her body. She was overcome by panic, and had to hide her flushed ears, and her eyes as they admired Haluk Bey, lowering her head to an imaginary nosebag. She couldn't listen. She was speaking fast to conceal her thoughts, describing the day the family went fishing in Salim Bey's fibreglass motorboat: the motionless sea, how Salim Bey and Billur Hanım tried to seduce the fish in the sea, the köfte sandwiches she'd prepared for the people in the boat, how in fact her mind remained with the sea, how the smooth water was split in two by the boat, how sometimes forgetting her work, she hung overboard from her waist to see the huge jellyfish which fed on pollution, the shoals of horse-mackerel, the terrifying rocks at the bottom: in short, all that was hidden in the blue... when she was speaking of the sea Nilüfer was full of an energy that overflowed to her listener. Haluk Bey surprised them both with the following offer:

'One day I'll take you to the seaside, if you like.'

Nilüfer felt weak and on fire like the flaming sunset, and bowed her head humbly as though to indicate 'anything you say'. They sat on the steps in silence. A youngish woman who knew her place and the man who was sowing seeds of hope in her heart.

To Nilüfer it seemed a month, to Haluk Bey a day, but in real time, free of emotion, it was only one hour before the neighbourhood watch let them know that the path was clear again.

It was time to move. Then a strange thing happened. In some indefinable way Haluk Bey was brought closer. It was Nilüfer's numb leg – all pins and needles – heavy as marble, that bridged the deep social gulf between them, and Haluk Bey held out his hand to Nilüfer. Love leapt like a spark from the hand of this regal man into Nilüfer's. And the days to follow would be described in the language of love.

Wrist

The lonely morning hours. Nilüfer was gathering the bite-sized cherry tomatoes from the green centre of the garden. In the mansion they were all sound asleep, their sleep intensified by the humidity. Her hands full of the garden's abundance, she hurried to the kitchen where she polished up the teapot before brewing the tea, then arranged the cushions, which she'd stowed under the eaves in case it rained, on the wicker chairs on the terrace, and on the glass plate she sliced the full-fat cheese she'd bought from the market. She knew every corner of the house like the palm of her hand.

The tea, sugar, coffee and all the kitchen paraphernalia in rows of glass jars aligned according to size… she knew the history of how every tablecloth that her mistress had forgotten came into the house: she knew the design of the cane set of furniture by the balcony door that led to the garden, and the seascape hanging in the centre of the bedroom wall that she looked at whenever she could steal a moment from cleaning. She too was part of the house, like the furnishings of the villa. A fixture. If she was gone even for a little while it was immediately noticed, like bread missing from the table.

Before the occupants of the house honoured breakfast with their presence, Nilüfer drank her tea tête-à-tête with the island. Two cups of tea were the only luxuries of her day.

But that day the tea didn't taste as usual. Since Haluk Bey had shown up, a different atmosphere breathed around the villa. She was seeing the world through his eyes. She craved for coffee like him, and like him she was beginning to feel nostalgia for the country – the city-dweller's longing to lie in the fields – and carried away by illusion, she began to imagine she was assimilating English from A to Z. If she opened her mouth she would suddenly become a grieving nightingale singing in English. She wondered if the affliction known as love was anything like what she was suffering. When she was aware of that jellyfish coiled up in her stomach, she would lean against every door Haluk Bey entered. When Billur Hanım's son was in the kitchen she would linger at the counter and become a glass of water, and when he sat on the terrace she became a brush and would clean the newly-swept terrace again, and she wouldn't wait for sunset but would hurry to the garden to water the flowers.

When he lingered a long time in the bathroom she missed him so much she could hardly stop herself opening the door on the pretext of fixing the toilet paper.

What things flooded her heart? They stopped her from working, eating, sleeping. She almost forgot her own name. In the narrow dark trousers she hadn't worn for years and the aubergine top that suited her freckled skin, she drifted aimlessly about the neighbourhood. In her daydreams she saw Haluk Bey's wrist as he struck the ball.

She used to compare the island house to a witch's castle. Now it troubled her that everything had taken on a different meaning. She was forgetting how contemptibly she'd been treated in this house she had entered at eighteen, the scoldings she'd had from the day she started work, and what her mistress had said when she poured the bleach through the tea-strainer. And at the age of almost thirty she was still a virgin.

And how many sleepless nights she had suffered from

the tactless things Billur Hanım had said before her guests. 'I lay the tablecloth I brought from Egypt and Nilüfer takes it off. What do you imagine was in her head – did she think that my beautiful table shouldn't be covered? If these people stay in one situation for any length of time, they begin to want the upper hand and insist on their rights. After ten years our one began to get above herself. Give them an inch and they take a mile.' When she went on like that, Nilüfer was already writing her letter of resignation in her head. But love conquered and overcame her annoyance. Nilüfer was like softened dough, worked on by the yeast.

She wanted Haluk Bey to keep her desire warm. His face, fingers, mouth; eating, being silent, opening for love; his lips whispering of far-off lands, and his badminton arm. Nilüfer carried his empty coffee cups back to the kitchen. But her eyes refused to cross the threshold. They stayed glued to Haluk Bey's badminton arm; to his strong wrist, developed by sport. His wrist movements reminded her of the elegance of handmade chests beside the crass crudity of ready-made furniture. She mooned around Haluk Bey all day like cats that haunt the butchers' shops.

Stomach

For Billur Hanım the plunge into the tumultuous Thursday crowd, which gathered just in front of the district office, was as good as going to Istanbul. Especially near noon when the crowd got denser. As the path opened for her between the congested stalls, in the hoarse voices of the market traders touting their wares, in the fruits of all colours that weighed down the scales, in every new path that revealed their dizzying variety, and in the crowds sworn not to come home without the best bargain; in all of this, she felt the rapid beat of Istanbul's pulse.

The traders from Yalova[1] had set up their stalls early, and were eyeing the islanders' way of pouring fresh vegetables mixed with fruit into tins, coffee pots, and decorated kitchenware. The neighbourhood echoed with young schoolboys shouting 'Carts available'. They'd carry the customers' baskets up the island's steep ramps, a task that required a good strong pair of lungs. As she piled up the boxes of tomatoes and grapes in the handcart, Billur Hanım realized she had lost count of her shopping and had bought too much. She was thinking of her son who would soon turn up on the island, and at the same time having a kilo of petals weighed, delicate as lace. Ah, Kalçunya![2] She'd forgotten the almond cake. Nilüfer was sent post-haste to the island's pâtisserie. 'Hurry up, Nilüfer dear,' said Billur Hanım, who could sweet-talk when she liked. 'We forgot my Haluk's special treat.'

The unwilling Nilüfer, one foot forward, the other lagging behind, set off for the patisserie. If she'd had any inkling of the future she wouldn't have complained. She was thinking, 'One more mouth to feed in the army of the hungry in this house.'

Sometimes life was so demanding.

But as soon as she stepped indoors she completely changed her mind. She would have run to the pâtisserie a thousand times to relive the moment when Haluk Bey took the packet from her hand with such pleasure; on the flight, he said, what he'd missed most were the island's special pastries. He practically fell on the fig tarts. It was so good to be acknowledged! To be met by Haluk Bey's innocent smile, which had never been sullied by the uncouth filth of this world! Nilüfer's eyes shone.

The market shopping had gone badly for Billur Hanım, whose arms had turned to jelly and now hung useless. Leaving the room to the young ones, she escaped to the bathroom to hide her annoyance.

1. Yalova – A city south of Istanbul on the eastern coast of the Sea of Mamara.
2. Kalçunya – A traditional Greek pastry.

Finally, at midnight when the inhabitants of the house were asleep and the neighbouring streets were deserted, Nilüfer was able to confront that strange feeling she had experienced. All day his eyes were veiled behind his laughter. Her body would not be able to endure this torment much longer. Her temperature rose to 39?

Next week, without a murmur, she was rolling out the puff pastries of meat and cheese. She was spreading the dough with her rolling pin and while it was thinning she inwardly repeated the English words she'd promised herself to learn. Don't ask where it came from, this desire to learn English instead of serving perfectly browned pastries. The class Nilüfer belonged to not only decreed the quantity of possessions she could own, but profoundly shaped the kind of relationship she could have with another. She couldn't foresee that her love of English might lead her into absurd situations. On the contrary, she thought it was child's play to jump on the trampoline of knowledge and rise to the heights she longed for. This naïve belief had led her to dive head-first into the English business. Like everyone else in the house she could manage English more or less in two weeks, perhaps two months. So she thought.

To reinforce the word '*stomach*' she repeated it aloud a few more times. But the baking tray was almost full. Distracted by the tapping of the rolling pin, she couldn't concentrate thoroughly on the lesson and while she was fixing the words in the English grammar book in her head, at the same time she was making a tour of Haluk Bey's face. '*Mouth*', '*lips*', '*nose*'… If love hadn't distracted her, perhaps her work would have been easier, but everything her five senses perceived led her back to Haluk Bey. Haluk Bey's mouth, Haluk Bey's eyelashes, Haluk Bey's nose…

Her ear caught Billur Hanım's voice. 'Overnight she became the old Nilüfer,' she was telling the household. The very idea that her condition could activate channels of acid in her stomach set her insides on fire. Thanks to Haluk Bey she was becoming sensitive to her stomach. Ever since the impertinent young man had increased the island's population by one, her gut was either sour or burning, and at night when she thought of him she writhed with cramps.

This time her insides went sour because English words wouldn't come into her head.

What was that English word for 'mide'?

She emptied the rubbish and with the rubber shoes on her feet (produce of the market) she approached the house as quiet as an angel.

'*Stomach.*' She reflected that the devious language of that distant island had created problems. Two hard consonants, a hissing 's' and a chubby 't', didn't sit prettily back-to-back in her mouth. What an elegant word 'mide' was, smooth as butter. Moreover, if you asked Nilüfer, between the word '*stomach*' and 'mide' there was no harmony at all.

If she could concentrate on the book she was holding, perhaps life would be easier, but when thoughts of Haluk Bey were added to the foreign language sessions, her memory worked well on the level but left her on the hill.

Mouth

Sunset on Panjur Street meant the ragged pink of oleander, the cyclamen colour of bougainvillea, the fresh green of the tea gardens and the reddish colour secreted by the eucalyptus tree in its trunk.

The yellow of the daisy, of the pine pollen, of the mimosas; the monarch of all yellows, all the tones of pink, the degrees of grey, the splashes of purple and a handful of dark blue, harbinger of evening.

As the sun continued to sink to the horizon, Nilüfer examined his mouth. It was the fourth week since he'd arrived. The joker of the mansion was opening and closing his mouth. Like a suction cup she grasped words, chewed them politely, rolling the crumbs down her throat, until she heard that word of three syllables, her own name: 'Nilüfer, come and look at this.'

Haluk Bey was pointing to the sun setting out on its melancholy journey over the island hilltops. Nilüfer couldn't get enough of looking at his mouth crammed with words: even if they weren't about the sunset, they poured into the world syllable by syllable and she noticed again the shape of his lips, bright pink as though they'd just come from a painter's brush. Till then she'd been deaf, but now suddenly her ears opened, as though she'd lent the words to someone and instantly they'd all come back. And while Haluk Bey went on at the centre of that divine scene, with his long sentences, Nilüfer changed back to her other self, and as he was enjoying the sunset, she rushed to empty two cups of water into the body of the coffee machine. It was very important to her that her own little hands should be involved.

As the man sipped his coffee, he caught something like the sadness of sunset in Nilüfer's mood. In her hair as it flamed in the sunset, in the way she looked at one with eyes tired from a day that was ending; a dark melancholy, indescribable, that seeped into the flavour of the coffee he held in his hand...

Some things are always being added or removed from the picture of love.

Love always consists, in a way, of these gains and losses. What they had felt together about sundown on the island and its indefinable spell, had changed Nilüfer. Haluk observed her freckles, so appropriate to the summer heat, little dots sprinkled over her shoulders and face like a light make-up. An attractive naturalness compared with the repulsive artifice of the women he knew. Suddenly he was in the mood. Now the young son of the house had entered the story physically.

This game, the hunting game, a little less wild than

nature's, but one to which he was accustomed, was a refuge
he had sought unsuccessfully. Now the game of catch-if-you-
can had begun, and he felt like those children who seldom
left the city and fell on a few plums on a branch by the
roadside, as though they'd never seen such things before. It
made the summer worthwhile.

He accompanied Nilüfer to empty the rubbish. The
deserted white mansion, its balcony occupied by crows, a
typical island house with the bay window overhanging the
street, an abandoned lodge, which became history from the
spark of a moment ... They reached the foot of the hill where
Nilüfer got rid of the rubbish. Two local ladies of Panjur
Street were discussing the weather. The eye-catching one
with the silver waistcoat grumbled, 'It don't half change fast!'
and the other agreed, 'Wot a mornin', but just see now!'

They returned, inhaling deep draughts of the smell of
honeysuckle.

One last time. Lips opened and closed. Then and there
Nilüfer realized that she loved this face in any language in the
world. Even if she couldn't master English or speak a single
word of the language to him, her longing sighs would still
continue. And yet, if only she could say something like *your
mouth and the sun*, or even better, proclaim her love in lines of
English poetry. Come on, let's give her a hand. Imagine if she
could pour out,

'*At the violet hour, the evening hour that strives*

Homeward, and brings the sailor home from sea,'
then things might speed up.

But never in her life could Nilüfer find words like those.

Haluk's face was creased in a frown, not like someone
contemplating pleasant thoughts, but like someone planning
to lay a trap. He grasped his cheek as though he wanted to
clutch the very roots of his teeth in his hand.

'My tooth hurts,' he said. 'What's 'wisdom' tooth in
Turkish? It's rotten, I guess.'

Quick-witted Nilüfer solved the problem. 'The one at

the back? The yirmi yaş tooth,' she said.

And now they began to enjoy comparing the English and Turkish words for Haluk's sore tooth. Haluk Bey couldn't explain why the English '*wisdom tooth*' should be named 'the twenty-year-old' tooth in Turkish, nor could Nilüfer explain the Turkish for the tooth which sooner or later bothers us all, even though it doesn't appear till we're twenty.

'So,' said Haluk, 'if my tooth is going to be pulled out soon, I'll be neither wise nor young.'

Nilüfer giggled. She didn't notice the implication of his words. She could have listened to him for ever, talking in any language in the world.

Eyes

They had just returned from the beach. That day the water was cleaner than it had been for weeks. Even Haluk swam, who for fear of jellyfish hadn't dipped a toe in the water since he arrived.

They showered. Wet bathing costumes and dirty towels were entrusted to Nilüfer on the quay. They were all as hungry as wolves.

The usual things happened; far out a sailing boat went by, seagulls began the day with their usual shrill screams and the sun dutifully warmed the garden, first the back then the front. Between meals, Haluk passed the time in the hammock, enclosed like a tent by the pine trees, turning the pages of the same kind of books with the same kind of subjects, none very serious. Nothing unexpected would shake life from its usual routine, no accident or disaster would spoil the monotony.

Perhaps one should stay close to the fire. For some time he had noticed the change in Nilüfer's attitude. So did he have to feed the fire? It was better than dying of boredom. He sprang up from the hammock and landed by Nilüfer, like a stone.

Now, when Nilüfer hears him say, 'I'm going for a little walk, do you want to come too?' just imagine how she feels.

She was grateful for her healthy physique that she didn't capsize, but her soul fell into a sad state.

She was smiling. A nervous smile. A grimace that revealed a struggle to control herself. The thought of Billur Hanım losing her son to Nilüfer caused an involuntary titter that was dying to turn into a laugh.

As they walked, the whoops from the ferryboat sirens were dispersed into the blue arch of the sky. From the quay, a warm breeze blew away announcements which landed at their feet.

'Some people are like the island,' said Haluk, 'they're loners and can't communicate with others. They're better with wind and water. And some are just the opposite, they can't set foot on the island. Many of my friends are like that, their souls can't stand the isolation of an island.'

On the way that wound down from Panjur Street to Pervane the man she desired was beside her with his hand and arm, with all his body and inaccessibility. Nilüfer swallowed him with her eyes. Haluk had no objections, he too was diving head-first into Nilüfer's eyes. He knew that salvation didn't lie that way. For there were depths, immeasurable depths that leave you paralysed, with no choice.

Pitiless depths.

He descended two more metres, and right at the bottom he met his mother and he admitted she was right, to give her her due. She's not my equal. We shouldn't plunge to depths we can't survive, it would be an irrecoverable disaster.

Suddenly Haluk Bey's eyes changed… He announced he would go to America sooner than expected. And Nilüfer wasn't able to ask why.

The world had rules.

Love had rules.

It wasn't up to them to change the rules.

Nilüfer was like a broken branch that can't bear the weight of snow heaped upon it; shouldn't one take note of the tree that can't refuse the ivy climbing over its trunk, or of the leaves obedient to nature in autumn?

That moment she made up her mind. She would bring the unattainable within reach.

If Haluk Bey had been able to guess his little companion's intentions, wouldn't he have preferred his boredom to a walk?

Face

Panjur Street was alarmingly silent. While everyone slept, Nilüfer's thoughts sneaked into his room like a wind whirling through his window with its opened shutters. She felt the bed whose sheet she had changed with her own hands. So this was love. This ignorance and lack of self-knowledge. To pitch a tent opposite parts of the body and just sit there. To touch that body in dreams. To give it uninterrupted attention from end to end until it cries, 'What's happening to me?'

Life was dangling over Nilüfer's mouth like delicious grape clusters descending from heaven. Past, present and future were in that room, gleaming in his body.

She couldn't take her eyes off Haluk's face, from his chest rising and falling with rhythmic breaths, or from his legs, legs like a waterway lit up by street lanterns. Lights pierced the deep blue of night. There she saw the reflections of police patrolling and tourists strolling idly by. As her eyes roamed over his body's contours, she was enjoying the pleasure of possessing a man who lay asleep, dead to the world. She touched his eyes, drowsy with sleep, and his defenceless body on the bed. As she stroked his wrists, and glued her eyes to the groove of his lip, there was no escape for the man who feared his heart might be taken from him.

But conscience knew their love was unsuitable, and warned her to turn away.

She dwelt for a long time on his wide-apart eyebrows. She kissed the dimples that caved in when he smiled. And standing there watching the presence she would soon lose, she realised there was something other than wealth that she wanted. It was Haluk Bey's own self. She knew for the first time that she was able to bring the man so close to her because she could love him, not in parts but as a whole.

Sleep.

To be able to possess the man, to love him with all her heart, she must know about sleep and how to make him cross its threshold. Only then could she possess the body she loved, for ever and completely. Nilüfer stepped back from the brink.

The weather was the same summer weather, the same cursed damp from the mountains creeping by night into the livers of the islanders. The same old stringing the beans and cracking them apart. But Nilüfer had changed. While the morning prayer was being recited, in an island mansion there was a woman who was going to make the world acknowledge her desire, however much it cost.

She would show the world what she could create with her passion. It came into her head during their walk. It couldn't wait. She would make it happen. She would carry out her idea and keep a part of him with her for ever.

On her day off, she went away to the island of Kınalı, mulling over the memories of her former life. The gently sloping garden of the old sculptor's country estate, the outhouses where the dear old watchman sheltered, the peach trees and mulberry bushes in the orchard. Remembering, she grieved for the years wasted there with him. But for once in her life, Nilüfer wished to make up for the hardships of her past.

'*Hands can carve up a person, hands can speak of our loneliness, hands can be a part of love.*' Isn't that what he had said? She was going to visit the sculptor who lived alone, summer and winter, on the island slopes open to the north wind, who worked alone, ending the day without having uttered a single word, and considered those moments when he wasn't being creative a waste of time.

Faces and hands; reshaped with every love, changed with every touch.

Nilüfer was lucky to find the artist still resident on the island. She hurried through the deserted streets of Kınalı.

The artist who for a long time had found his loneliness unbearable was delighted at Nilüfer's visit, and tried everything to make her stay a little longer. Although he had lost his looks, he tried his luck with any young woman who happened to come his way. 'I wonder what's happened in your life,' he said.

But she gave him no encouragement. He wanted to do a charcoal drawing of Nilüfer, but 'I haven't the time,' she said.

'You're my guest, I'm at your service. Stay and let's make the most of what God sends us,' he insisted.

Again she took no notice, then the old sculptor's voice, rough with nicotine, suddenly asked, 'What would you like to do?' Nilüfer squirmed and, evading the question, cunningly led him round to the subject of the garden.

'Nature here hasn't changed,' he said, 'perhaps the weeds have grown a bit more, and the vine that smothers the trellis is stronger. Everything else is the same.'

She narrowed her eyes. 'We don't have all the time in the world like you people,' said Nilüfer, 'There's work. There's the lady of the house,' she hesitated, 'and there's the son of the house….' For him to be always with her was what Nilüfer wanted. Even if it was only in parts.

Nilüfer made her final request to the artist, who was on the threshold of old age.

'For years I dealt with your letters. I was the one who found you the best clay, I was the one who mixed your plaster-of-Paris. Now do me a favour and, without asking too many questions, tell me how to carry out the thing you said was "so simple, my dear", how to make a mask of someone's face.'

They were in the laundry room on the top storey. Haluk and Nilüfer. She looked at him. Once more. Again and again, hovering about him. He had come on the ridiculous pretext of asking her to iron his shirt. While he knowingly pulled it over his head, undid the buttons and wickedly peeled the slightly sweaty garment off his skin, she prayed he would fall and his life become a prison, and he would need her care for weeks on end. And all the while she was still doing her duty. She took the shirt. And when she allowed him to touch her arm jokingly with a man's usual boldness, the touch set her blood on fire. This she allowed, because eventually she was going to send him to sleep, not with curses and evil wishes but with a glass of water.

It was the best phase of the work. The most exciting moment of the whole summer.

While he slept, surrendering to sleep like an innocent, defenceless child, even the shadow she worshipped was hers.

He was hers. Her willing model.

Master and servant had exchanged roles. She laid him down. As he lay there like a dead man she watched him, holding her breath, reckoning that the effect of the drug would last another five or six hours. She must move fast. Every passing moment was working against her.

It was difficult.

God had given the man the beauty of water. Nilüfer could hardly control her palms. But as she covered his eye sockets with them, her fingers wandered over his eyelids and she was reminded of the winding paths of the island. When she found the groove of his mouth she felt like a hedgehog. She crossed her arms and drew in her head and became a little ball.

Ahh! There she wouldn't go near. When she took his hands in hers his muscles contracted in spasm. Haluk was dead to the world. He was asleep, captive of a woman's desire that gradually grew and spread. One by one Nilüfer drew out the knives of desire from her body.

The next step was to touch his back. There by the ironing board she embraced him (how often she had dreamt it!). She felt light, wandering the island on the crest of trees, jumping from the tip of one pine to another. She was leaping round her lover, free of rough work like sweeping floors and shaking rugs. She had assumed the form of a beautiful djinn.

She couldn't stand it. One by one she undid his shirt buttons. Only moments remained before the contact with his skin she had imagined for weeks. She closed her eyes, afraid. She leant over his body. He was on fire and the heat of his core poured into Nilüfer's body.

So, by the end of two hours when they lay together she had taken possession of him, she had assimilated the bones that shaped his face, the cartilage that shaped his nostrils, every single pore, until her eyes collapsed in their sockets. Even their palates and eye sockets exchanged places. Now she was Haluk. She looked at the world through his eyes.

Where she was heading was dangerous. Nilüfer had turned aside from her goal. For one last time she touched the man's face. While he slept, the light of loneliness fell on his face. He was unaware that this light – and the anatomical facial structure peculiar to himself – was in the possession of a woman.

She mixed the plaster of Paris to a creamy thickness and, following the maestro's instructions, smeared Vaseline on the unconscious man's eyebrows. She would make a mould of his face. Vaseline was essential to prevent plaster sticking to the skin and facial hair remaining in the plaster. Starting at the chin, she smeared a fine layer of plaster over the whole face, on forehead, cheeks, eyelids. Then as it was setting quickly she moved on to further layers. 'You must take care that the cast is not too thin, or it will distort and you won't be able to get it off.' Working fast, she went over in her mind the sculptor's instructions: 'The more delicately you work, the more accurate the shape will turn out.' Surely that's what he said.

When the first layer dried to a skin she proceeded to the second and third layers. Then she had to turn back from under the corner of the eye, the cheekbone and under the chin. 'Imagine you're pouring plaster into a cognac glass with a narrow mouth.' the maestro had warned her. You won't be able to remove the plaster without breaking the glass: the human face is such that if you go towards the ear you can't remove the cast in one piece.

The little details of practical information given her by the wretched sculptor, like the length of time the plaster took to cool, and the plastic tube stuck in the nostrils to facilitate breathing, were immensely useful as she carried out her project. Without his advice she wouldn't have known black from white, but thanks to him it would all be as easy as putting a tin of beans on the stove.

If only excitement wouldn't distract her and make her clumsy. A privilege to be able to touch him, the mind-boggling flesh... In her desire to remove the mould she cracked the plaster. It must have been put on too thin. But she was sure she had done everything to the letter. Back to square one.

She began at the chin, smearing on the plaster and pausing at the aching wisdom tooth. She touched it and thought he might be awake. *I wonder if it aches while he is sleeping?* She rubbed her cheek as though her own tooth was sore. One more layer of plaster.

She was startled by the heat the cast gave off. She had forgotten that the ice-cold plaster would warm up in time, a sign that everything was going in the right direction and that the negative was ready. For a moment she panicked, thinking that Haluk was stirring in his sleep. She still had to clean the inside of the negative with soap and water, and pour plaster in its liquid form into it to make the model. And she must slip away at the latest before Billur Hanım returned from her game of bridge.

Clearing up and bringing everything back to its original

state would take half an hour. She must not leave any traces or Billur Hanım might go to the police and accuse her of stealing. She thought fast as she wiped off the Vaseline with soap and water. Whatever happened, the struggle would be worthwhile. For once, love would be on her side.

But things were not going well, something was absent. The beauty enhanced by the power of love, the mysterious meaning of a man's eyes, the noble whiteness of his skin, his mouth indescribable as the well of desire, the provoking curl of his lips, in short all that Nilüfer thought of as Haluk's attractions was missing.

The island's gentle air, the quiet hours of Panjur Street, were not woven into the fabric of the mask. Love's ardour, its power to make a paper bird fly, had not been poured into the plaster.

Nilüfer had been sure that all those lines and shadows of care and anxiety in the man's face would pass into the portrait, but it had not turned out as she hoped.

The cast had been made, her wish fulfilled. She stood alone on a hilltop on the island, holding the mask that was meant to immortalize her beloved's face. She was looking at the mask of an ordinary man. She went on waiting for it to reveal a miracle, for her desire to flare up, to catch fire.

But there was nothing.

The man was still where he'd cast anchor three months ago like a ship tethered safely to the harbour. Still there.

And Nilüfer was alone with her obsession.

His divine beauty – the essence that Nilüfer had failed to capture – had come to an end, reduced to that mask.

Love was still out of reach.

A hand remained, a face, and the end of a dream.

Translated by Ruth Christie

Marked in Writing

Murat Gülsoy

"...KIMBERLY TOOK A deep drag from her cigarette, her eyes fixed on Adams. She wasn't going to speak. As she waited for him to say the first word, she prepared herself for the full-blown fight about to erupt, a fight that would begin with an innocent question: 'What did you do today?' or 'How was work?' It was difficult dealing with Adams' fits of jealousy, now an integral part of their daily hell. She didn't know how much longer she could keep it up. Kimberly was busy lighting up yet another of the cigarettes she'd been smoking non-stop all evening, when Adams tossed his head back, sending chunks of ice rolling from his glass into his mouth, and began crunching away. She thought to herself that it was only towards one's husband that a person could possibly feel such a groundless sense of guilt. As Adams loosened his tie, he asked in a tender voice the question that would start the fight and end with Kimberly getting a black eye. 'What did you do today, Sweetie?' Kimberly's lower lip was already trembling. What *hadn't* she done in the eyes of this sick man old enough to be her father... As soon as he turned his back..."

All of a sudden the lamp next to my bed went dead. Trying not to lose my page, I placed the book on the empty pillow next to me. Kimberly could wait. Although it was obvious to me that the electricity had gone out, I nevertheless groped around in the dark, trying to find the lamp switch. Once I did, I fiddled around with it for a bit, but to no avail – it was a bona fide blackout. I tried to guess what time it was.

I'd arrived home around half past midnight. It had been nearly half an hour since I'd gotten into bed and started reading. When the electricity went out at an hour like that, there was no telling when it would come back on. Plenty of people must have been sound asleep in bed. Even if there were others like me, suffering from a bout of insomnia, they wouldn't go to the trouble of letting the electric company know about the blackout. After all, they were just going to sleep anyway. I headed for the window, to see how widespread the blackout was.

There was a dense fog outside. And the street lamps were out. The apartment blocks across the way that I was used to seeing from this angle were rendered invisible by the fog and the darkness. I waited in vain for a car to pass through the avenue, finally giving up hope. I knew that Monday nights were the most boring, deadest time of the week in this city. When I opened the window to get some fresh air, my throat was attacked by a cold, smoky darkness that seared my nasal passages. I closed the window. I leaned my legs against the radiator, trying to get warm. But the radiator was quickly growing cold. I couldn't decide what to do next. I could get back into bed and wait for sleep to come, or I could seek a source of light.

As I headed to the kitchen, feeling my way along, I recalled that I didn't have any candles, neither the little white ones they sold at corner stores nor the decorative variety found in abundance in every home these days. After wandering around in the darkness like a blind ghost for a while, it occurred to me: in the emergency bag which I had prepared in case of an earthquake, but which I had soon after abandoned to oblivion in a closet drawer, there would be a flashlight. When I finally managed to find the flashlight, I pushed down on the button only to see the filament of the bulb turn red and then the battery expel its final breath. The way the light went on and off so quickly in the pitch black darkness dazzled my eyes so much, that I couldn't be sure the bulb had actually lit up at all or not. Maybe I'd just imagined it. The only thing for certain was that the darkness continued. I put the bag back where I'd fetched it from and returned to bed.

For a while I closed my eyes and tried to sleep. The room was so dark I couldn't tell whether my eyes were shut or not. I was thinking, *If only I had a match or a lighter*, when the image of me tossing my Zippo into one of the most unsightly drawers of my desk at the office the other day flashed before my very eyes. That moment of stupor when I began to implement my decision to give up smoking and all of its accessories. Yet now, what I wouldn't have given for a smoke... There was a pack of tobacco around here somewhere, forgotten in some corner, I was sure of it... But even if there was, what would I have lit it with anyway? I used an electric stove; another reason not to keep any matches or lighters around. I had surrendered myself completely to civilization.

I just couldn't manage to fall asleep. As I rolled around in bed in exasperation, I found my nose buried in the book that I'd forgotten there on the pillow a few minutes ago. (Me and an open book in a double bed.) Kimberly must have already taken that punch. But then why was I reading this book that did nothing but escalate my exasperation... Human relationships that remained unresolved, depressing depictions of the city, tired psychological analyses... I should give up reading such novels, I thought. After all, they were really nothing but poor variations of my own life, bereft as it was of subtlety and aesthetics. When I turned over, the book fell onto the floor, making such a terrible noise that I was suddenly awoken from my slumber. It was only then that I realized I'd been drifting between being awake and asleep for some time. And then I had this feeling that when the book hit the floor, a thief must have taken advantage of the situation and broken into the flat, and that now he was slyly waiting for a second burst of noise so that he could make his next move. I sat up in bed and began listening to the flat. Not a peep. There wasn't the slightest sign of a living being, except for the sound of my own breath and heartbeat. This exaggerated silence stoked the fear of the primitive man within me. If only a car would drive down the avenue, at the very least... Sure, I could understand why people weren't wandering about the streets in the middle of the night on a Monday, but still... (but wasn't *this* much silence a bit odd?) And then, a nightmare I'd had years ago suddenly came to life in the timeless space of the subconscious.

Unlike the intense darkness surrounding me, the nightmare began on a sunny evening. I was walking through the streets of my neighbourhood. Everything was pretty much as it is in real life. Except for one detail: the streets weren't made of asphalt or stone. All of the roads were covered in desert sand that had come from who knew where. And so I was walking on the warm sand, this sand that covered everything, staring at it in awe. By the time I noticed the false teeth strewn over the sand dune, much like the oyster shells I was used to seeing along the shore, the dream was already quickly en route to becoming a nightmare. The feeling of dread growing inside of me bore with it another piece of information: In these homes, on these streets, in this neighbourhood, in this city, there was NO ONE. Everyone had either died or run away. There was no one left but me. (The teeth must have belonged to the deceased.) I had woken up at a point when I could no longer bear the abstract feeling of loneliness. It was years ago. I remembered it like it was yesterday, how I had woken up in a students' house, which we'd tried to heat using a coal stove, and lit a short, filterless cigarette, and how the acid in my stomach had risen to my mouth and sent this burning sensation through my nasal passages. Despite the decades that had passed. The decades that had passed for naught...

The seemingly endless darkness combined with the negative thoughts in my head to make sleep nearly impossible. But I needed to go to sleep right away. I placed a pillow beneath my head for support and decided to start all over again. I was going to take the foetal position, without bunching part of the blanket between my legs, without turning left and right, just lying there, motionless. If I didn't budge, sleep would automatically accumulate in my muscles and eventually reach my mind. After that, my brain, weary from the lack of motion, would usher me through the gate that led to my dreams. This was an effective method that I had developed for sleepless nights. In addition to these physical measures, I could try to imagine one of the pleasant dreams recorded in my memory, in order to stave off the daily thoughts harassing my mind. This method resembled trying to ladle a little water into a pump that had been out of order for a long time. I had to inject a portion of dream into my mind using a ladle.

In one of the pleasant dreams I'd had recently, I'm taking a nighttime stroll through the back streets of Hisar. When I arrive at the square with the big plane tree, suddenly everything turns dark. Not only are the homes and the streets buried in darkness, but the stars in the sky too suddenly become invisible. As if a huge, dark cloud is rolling right over them. I continue walking for a while, unable to see where I'm stepping. But it turns out that a bunch of tables have been set up on the square, where they've erected some sort of outdoor pub. At one of the tables beneath the tree sit a bunch of friends from the area where we had our summer house, where I'd spent my summers as a teenager. They recognize me and call out to me. We're over here, come here, they say. I'm so happy. As I begin walking towards them, the clouds part and the stars come out, shinier than ever. The city is so dark that the stars look as close and huge as they did the night of the big earthquake. So much so, in fact, that the light of each star falls upon the face of the earth in a narrow beam. The bundles of rays coming from what seem like miniature spotlights, illuminate the sand where we are. My friends had brought the sand with them, from the place where we'd spent

63

our summers. Filled with happiness, I watch the bouquets of light emanating from the stars. I stick my hand out, slipping it through each ring of light. Just then, I hear a sound, like the whizzing sound you hear in science fiction movies. I understand that the light is much more powerful than it appears to be... People are lying about on the sand. They derive a sensual pleasure from the light touching their bodies. The light, it seems, fills and enriches our souls and our minds with something I can't quite identify. At first, I'm happy to have experienced this special moment. Then I become worried. I think that such strong beams of light coming from the depths of space could be harmful too.

The similarity that I recognized, as I quickly replayed this dream, escalated the fear within me and muddled my mind. Lights going out all of a sudden... The swift descent of darkness... Just like what happened now! (There must be a reason behind this coincidence.) I urged my mind into action, calling upon reason and logic for help. As my mental functions, which were not accustomed to working at this late hour of the night, announced the result of their emergency meeting, they didn't seem all that reliable. What they suggested was clear and precise: you're in a dream. You're experiencing a nightmare variation of the dream you had that night. I was trying with all my being to oppose this suggestion which, far from relieving me, only served to increase my horror: I never realize I'm having a dream while I'm having a dream! This can't be a dream. See, I'm touching the bed, the blanket, myself, and everything is solid, concrete. After nonchalantly listening to me, my weary mind and reason asked: can you prove that you're not having a dream?

Of course I couldn't prove it.

Tired of fighting, my exhausted mind was throwing in the towel. I could make one last move, get up, feel my way to the bathroom, wash my hands and face and pull myself together. That is, if the water was still running... I could hardly expect the water to make its way up to this floor on its own.

Maybe the blackout would be over in a little bit, and the bedside lamp would come on and start emitting light, as if nothing had happened, and I would continue reading the book from where I'd left off. I held my breath and began to wait. Now! No, now! Right now! Now...

Nothing happened, nothing at all, in the darkness, which continued to grow colder. Not a movement, not a sound. If only I could listen to some music at least. I'd been so caught off guard by this blackout... If only I had, for example, a battery powered radio, a battery lantern that would give off milky white light for a few brief hours, a few humble candles, a match, a pack of cigarettes, I could have very well turned this darkness into a pleasant night. But I had none of them.

Really, didn't I? Or was everything different from how I perceived it? I felt the existence of something evil, something I hesitated to speak of even.

(Actually, the electricity hadn't gone out. Actually, nothing was as I thought it was. Actually...) I was afraid. Very, very afraid. A meaningless, reasonless, illogical fear. Just like the fear I used to get when I was a child... Whatever that evil thing was there in my midst, a thing I could not yet define, I lie still as the dead in order not to upset it, in order not to draw its attention to me.

(Maybe I was dead.) That was an option. My weary mental faculties were laughing at me, tongue in cheek, but not without a slight expression of worry on their faces too. Maybe this is what death was like. A process that ends with you being buried in darkness all of a sudden, as if the electricity's been cut off. I saw, heard, felt nothing. I could no longer be certain that I was lying in a bed, and I could no longer imagine that I was having a nightmare. I had to get out of bed. Or I, as an adult on the verge of middle age, had to face my childhood fear, which had come back to life, triggered by a common blackout. I decided to think it all through again, starting from the very beginning.

I think it was the middle of first grade. I had stopped watching cartoons at the cinema on the weekends and started watching the latest westerns and karate films instead. The reason for these cinematic outings was the interest that my eldest uncle took in helping to bring me up, the son my family had eagerly awaited for so many years. According to my perception of him then, not of how I would analyze him now, he was an old man, who smelled of tobacco, wore a grey suit, and had a thin moustache and pepper gray hair. On one of those weekend outings, when our bus pulled up to the stop in front of Tan Cinema, which is long gone now, I started insisting that we go to this one particular film. Maybe I'd gotten tired of the karate films, maybe it was because of the muddy crowd there in Beyoğlu, I don't know, but I was adamant: we just had to go see *The Night of the Vampires*! When I read the title written on a dark poster in quivering red letters – so I could read at the time – I was overcome by this feeling that I just had to see that movie, and so I started yanking on my uncle's coat sleeve. And my uncle gave in and made the huge mistake of taking me to that film. Thinking back on it now... Neither the ticket sellers at the window nor the ushers tried to stop us from watching it. Yet that third rate horror movie would inflict deep wounds upon me.

I remember it clear as day: we were sitting towards the back of the cinema. In the first scene, the only sunny scene in the film, a woman and a man – whom I now understand were archaeologists – were talking about a vampire grave that had been unearthed amongst some ruins. Clearly this scene was shot to provide viewers with background knowledge, necessary because the scenario was so poorly written. When, in a display of unnecessary curiosity, the woman archaeologist tried to open the sarcophagus, one of the sharp stones scratched her hand and – wouldn't you know it – a few drops of blood dripped into the mouth of the vampire skeleton. The evil that had been hidden away beneath the earth for thousands of years would rise to the surface once again thanks to those few drops of blood. I don't recall exactly what happened after that, just that all the remaining scenes were of a bunch of vampires and werewolves shrouded in darkness. Creatures that were part animal part human, teeth growing longer and longer, pupils growing bigger and bigger, half naked vampire women... With my small hands I did my best to cover my eyes, but the sounds I heard kept me trembling in fear. I don't remember if we watched the film till the end or if we left in the middle, but what I had seen was enough to keep me from falling asleep on my own at night from then on.

At first my dad would sit at my bedside, quietly waiting for me to fall asleep. If he left the room before I did fall asleep, a huge werewolf would barge into my room, smashing the window of our third floor flat and causing me to break out in screams. How ridiculous those fears seem to me now, as I look around at the darkness surrounding me. But back then, my child's mind had difficulty separating fantasy from reality.

Finally one day my dad couldn't take it anymore and so he reprimanded my uncle. I don't think it was very common to take children to psychologists back then. 'You messed this kid up, now you fix him,' my father said, handing me over to my uncle. I don't what my uncle answered, or the thoughts that ran through his mind. The only thing I remember is that the following Saturday morning, instead of going to the cinema, we headed off to a different neighbourhood.

We'd been to Eyüp Sultan before. At the time it seemed like we hadn't been there for years, but in reality – doing the maths now – I know that it couldn't have been longer than a year, when I'd been taken there before starting school to learn 'elifba'[1]. According to my uncle, the member of our family responsible for upholding traditions, I had to sit cross-legged before Eyüp Sultan's muezzin and repeat the Arabic letters he showed me, so that Allah would grant me mental alertness, so that I wouldn't have trouble reading and writing, and so that

1. elifba – The Arabic alphabet.

I would be an erudite person. My childhood self, at the time equally indifferent to Arabic and Latin letters, had repeated the hodja's[2] words: Elif... elif... ba... ba... jim... jim... I don't recall how many letters we went over, of course. In fact, I'm not even sure we got to jim, but I am certain of the elif-ba pair. And so the Saturday morning when my father handed me over to my uncle for him to 'fix' me, we made our way to Eyüp Sultan.

The intervening thirty years has erased plenty from my memory, but that day I still remember well. The interesting thing is that I just realized I have never thought about that day until I started thinking about it now, a memory triggered by the fears brought on by the blackout. Or maybe I had thought about it... But when? When, I wonder, had I last opened the door to those memories? It was hard to tell. The image that appeared to me was something like this: a large mosque courtyard, a hexagonal or octagonal structure that I can easily say, even if we didn't go into it, was a mausoleum and a bunch of bearded men circumambulating it, amulets and prayer beads hanging from their hands... It was a sunny day. I remember that it wasn't very cold. Now, as far as my memory recalls, when I tried to breathe in the air there, I caught the scent of the handrails in the old Leyland buses, handrails worn down till they had a satin-like feel to them. And the scent of charcoal, familiar to me because it pervaded the room where I had sat cross-legged in front of the hodja... Perhaps these memories didn't reflect the truth exactly. My mind had most likely played tricks on me over time, projecting onto the screen a short film comprised of an amalgamation of details that I had encountered here and there and, making some sort of connection between them, had pieced together from the nameless corners of my mind. Or all of this had somehow happened at a speed my child's mind struggled to record, and I had gathered these bits from

2. hodja – Title of respect across the Middle East.

the sentences my uncle later spoke when reporting the situation to my mother.

My uncle said to the hodja, 'The child's been taken over by some sort of fear; he can't sleep at night. Is there a cure?' After exhaling a few prayers, the contents of which I was never able to learn, straight into my face, he said that it would require an amulet containing a powerful prayer, but that none of the con men circling around us – at this point he motioned towards the window looking onto the structure that I had taken to be a mausoleum – had such an amulet, that most of the amulets they sold contained nothing but blank pieces of paper, and that those which did contain writing were full of meaningless, inaccurate things that paved the path to sinful deeds. And then he spoke of someone else. A very important, very powerful man.

The man's store was located in Sahaflar Çarşısı, the antique book market. I remember that as soon as we set foot in the large, dimly lit antique bookstore, a group of old men sitting around a huge table in the middle of the room suddenly grew quiet and set their eyes upon me and my uncle. I recall that even my insufficient cognitive abilities told me at the time that things just kept getting more and more baffling. I could no longer conceive of what we were doing there. Or rather, I couldn't understand that what had dragged us to this mysterious shop in that big market full of black books, was a third rate horror film. I was unable to piece together what was happening.

The man that the hodja at Eyüp Sultan sent us to was an important tariqat[3] leader. But the man my uncle talked to wasn't one of those weird, bearded men in a turban that we're used to seeing on television these days. Like the others sitting around the table, he was a grave, clean-shaven man dressed in a suit and tie. Now my uncle told this man what had happened. Feeling myself shrink, feeling flawed, wrong, like a

3. tariqat – In Sufism: the pathway to enlightenment.

freak that had been taken over by evil spirits and was waiting to be saved, I hid behind my uncle. After hearing my uncle out, the stern man said, 'Take a walk and come back in an hour or two.' I don't remember him saying anything else. I recall that when we left the dimly lit room with the old men who held the forces of evil in their hands, I regained my composure, like audience members who relax and finally begin to rustle about in their seats when a bright scene comes on, following a dark, tense scene of a horror film. But I knew that we were going to go back there. And that fact told me that the film wasn't over yet.

We wandered around beneath a plane tree for a while. At that moment, I thought my uncle existed for me alone. Thinking about it now, I understand much better what a man taking the son of his much younger sister out for a walk in Beyazıt might have been experiencing. He was taking himself out too, no doubt. He must have gazed at the stands with the antique books where he had lived out his youth, or the pigeons flitting about, landing and taking flight from beneath the plane tree. All of a sudden he had gone from being a man who took his little nephew to the cinema, to someone in search of a mystical treatment for an unnamed disease. Maybe if he'd been married, if he'd had his own children, he would have been a completely different man. Maybe that's what he was thinking as he squeezed my little hands in his palm; I don't know.

We returned to the shop, taking solemn steps, a few hours later. The tariqat leader in the tie met us holding two small pieces of paper. He explained to my uncle: 'These are the last two pages of the zodiac. The child should carry them on his being at all times; it will do him good.' Overcome with curiosity, I glanced at the papers in the brief second before my uncle put them in his pocket. It was a spell consisting of two large circles made of Arabic letters, framed by writing, again in Arabic. It was the first and last time that I would see that writing.

When we got home, my uncle told my mum exactly

what the tariqat leader had said and then he took the papers with the spell from his pocket and began folding them. They wrapped the papers in a piece of nylon they'd found somewhere there at home, so that they wouldn't get water or sweat on them. Then they placed them in a tiny pouch made from an old undershirt of mine and stitched it together in a triangle. The spell had now taken a form that could be attached to the upper left side of my undershirt with a safety pin.

I barely remember what happened after that. Usually I forgot all about the amulet once I'd put my clothes on; once in a blue moon though, when I was about to get into a scrap with the villainous scoundrels in my class, I'd recall that I was wearing an amulet and think that I was different from the other kids. I'd think that I was a child who bore a mark, that I was marked in writing and wore the sign of a great divine force the source of which I did not know. Of course at the time I wasn't thinking in those words, but I believed that this amulet which was powerful enough to protect me from vampires and werewolves, protected me from lots of other things too, and that it even gave me a kind of superiority that I couldn't quite identify.

All of sudden the computer's printer started working, the electronic clock on the stove began to beep, and the bedside lamp came on, informing me that the electricity had returned. I opened my eyes.

For a moment, I really thought that a thief had been in the flat. The wardrobe door was open, my clothes were strewn all over the floor, and the room was in complete disarray. When I saw the earthquake bag lying lifeless on the floor, I realized in less than a tenth of a second that I was responsible for creating this mess, and I relaxed. I stared at the ceiling for a while and I asked myself why I had been so frightened. All of this couldn't have been just because of an untimely horror film. My frequent nightmares, my weird dreams... Was it because I no longer had my amulet? Or was it my lack of belief that scared me so? Maybe if I were a fervent believer, and I had an amulet to serve as my pact with that belief... (I wouldn't be afraid of going mad.) So when exactly had I ceased to believe? The day the amulet disappeared? Or during my high school years when I buried my nose in all those philosophy books and encyclopedias? Or during university, when I realized that the world was far from a just place? For real, just how had that amulet disappeared anyway?

The amulet, which had always been securely fastened to me, disappeared one morning. Though my mother and I looked all over the place for it, we were left empty-handed. We were both certain that I'd been wearing the amulet the night before. We turned my bed, my entire room upside down; we took the dirty clothes out of the washer and dumped them onto the floor, just in case, and searched the place from top to bottom. But it was nowhere to be found. Because I hadn't seen a sign of my fears for a long time, and because my uncle came and gave a mystical interpretation of what had happened, I didn't dwell on it. After listening to the story of the amulet's disappearance, my uncle spoke all-knowingly. 'It's disappeared because it has fulfilled its duty.' He was so sure of himself as he spoke those words, it was as if he said, 'There you have it, the greatest proof that it was a real amulet. If it hadn't been a real amulet, if we'd been tricked by those quacks in Eyüp Sultan, the amulet never would have disappeared, and it never would have banished my darling nephew's fears.'

I never had any fears of the kind again. I did still have the occasional worrying nightmare when I felt like I was the last person on earth, and those beautiful yet disquieting dreams in which I was marked by powerful beams of light that drifted down upon me from the stars. Maybe those teeth strewn along the city's streets belonged to my uncle; maybe the stars that decorated the night of my dreamworld with beams of light came from the last two pages of the zodiac, who knew...

When I got up to wash my face and have a drink of water, I stepped on the book that I'd knocked off the bed a short while before.

As I picked the book up from out of the sand that covered the floor, I said out loud, 'You're alright, aren't you, Kimberly?'

I disappeared from sight, there in the middle of the flat, without waiting for an answer.

Translated by Amy Spangler

The Intersection

Mehmet Zaman Saçlıoğlu

THE DOLMUŞES THAT leave from Kadıköy and go to Bostancı veer suddenly away from the shore as they round the point at Moda and turn into one of the district's somewhat older side streets. This street takes you down the hill to Moda, and from there to Yoğurtçu Park.

The street, which used to be very congested at several intersections, was not at all liked by dolmuş drivers coming up the hill. There were traffic lights at only two places here, one at the intersection with Moda Caddesi, the other at the intersection with Bahariye Caddesi. At the other intersections, young kids who had just got their driving licenses (and some that had not succeeded) created a hazard, showing off in their fathers' cars.

The experienced old dolmuş drivers, who drove cautiously, slightly hunched over the steering wheels of their aged, rattletrap cars, collecting fares and dispensing change, approached these hazardous intersections with their left foot on the clutch and their right poised to hit the brake at any moment.

One day a man started directing traffic at the most treacherous of the intersections. Although people were slightly taken aback at first, they soon grew accustomed to his presence. Clean-shaven, with glasses, a long raincoat and a whistle in his mouth, the man flawlessly executed the hand and arm movements of a bona fide traffic director – stopping cars and giving them the right of way, making all the cars wait for an elderly woman and then saluting her politely – and before long he was a fixture at the intersection.

The local shopkeepers, the neighbours who observed the proceedings from their windows and the drivers who regularly used the street, soon realized that the man was a harmless idiot. What else could he have been? What could a traffic director with no monthly salary, no rank, no social security, no weapon, no uniform and no forms for writing up tickets be other than an idiot?

It was, in all probability, the corner grocer who was the first to determine that this man, who stuffed a slice of kashar cheese into a half loaf of bread for lunch and attempted to direct the traffic on the one hand while eating his lunch on the other, was a nut job.

The first time he entered the shop, the man wished the grocer a polite good day, put in his order, and made a couple of gestures to the cars from a distance to show that he was on the job even as he stood waiting at the door of the grocery for his sandwich to be made. To the grocer, who asked him who he was and why he was directing traffic here, he replied: 'Can't talk now, I'm on duty.' He paid without taking his eyes off the street and, taking his sandwich, resumed his post in the middle of the intersection.

The grocer watched the man briefly and then got absorbed in his business. Towards evening, while he was waiting on a customer, he heard a horn-honk and looked for the man but was unable to discern anyone at the intersection. It surprised the grocer to see that this intersection, which had looked after itself for years, had abandoned its old habits and quickly adapted to the traffic director, only to revert to chaos again on his departure.

After the first few days, the traffic director's working hours fell into a regular pattern. With his whistle, his hand and arm movements and a smile on his face, the man, who took his place at the intersection at 7:30 in the morning, directed traffic without a break until five in the evening and disappeared at precisely 5pm. On Sundays the intersection was untended.

In the end, everyone came to accept the man, who observed his weekly working hours punctiliously and solved the traffic problem on the street. Now and then at midday while he was eating his lunch the man would utter a few words, but he never took his eyes off the traffic. He never made school children, pregnant women, or old people wait to cross the street but immediately stopped the cars, not giving the go sign until the pedestrians had reached the opposite kerb.

Before long the grocer stopped accepting money for the man's lunches. He felt indebted to this person who toiled with boundless energy and a smile on his face with no expectation of anything in return. In any case all the poor soul ate was half a loaf of bread and a hundred grams of kashar cheese.

'Why won't you take the money?' he asked. 'Am I a beggar?' The grocer was prepared for all possible questions.

'I beg your pardon, brother, but the Department of Traffic told me not to take money from their officer,' he said. 'They are very pleased with your work and they are going to pay for your lunches from now on,' he explained, quashing any further objections.

This reply prompted the man to take his work even more seriously, to the point of extending his workday by another hour. The grocer gave the same reply to questions about the man asked by people he didn't know who entered his shop as first-time customers

What do you mean an idiot, my good man? He is more intelligent than any of us. Some so-called great men take office saying they are going to administer the state and then make a hash of it. That man has been directing the traffic all this time without a hitch. He doesn't take a penny for it and he doesn't complain either. God knows, I can't tell who is crazy and who is sane. I used to have a shop boy. I paid him good money but he was lazy and a thief to boot. I couldn't even get him to work for tips. This man has invented a job for himself. Who in the world has ever seen a volunteer traffic director who worked without pay? Let the department of traffic come over here and see what a real traffic director is!

Some of the customers were taken aback and said, 'Well, if he's not an idiot, then what's he doing here?' And very few of them took a lesson from his example.

One noon when he was getting his lunch, the man took a folded piece of paper out of his pocket, unfolded it and handed it to the grocer.

'Would you mind putting this up in your shop window?'

'What does it say on that paper?' asked the grocer, and then he started reading it:

'Traffic director to be hired for this intersection. All those interested are requested to apply to Officer Cemil after six in the evening. Signed, Officer Cemil.' At the bottom was an enormous signature in scrawling letters.

'What happened? Are you leaving?' asked the grocer, saddened.

'Not for now,' replied the man. 'Actually I do have to go. On my way here this morning I saw an accident down below. There used to be a lot of accidents there as well, so it's even more hazardous than here. But it wouldn't be right to leave without finding somebody for here.'

'I see,' said the grocer. 'But let me write this in big letters for you. This is very small, it won't be noticed.'

The man was pleased and grinned from ear to ear.

'Okay,' he said. 'God bless you!' Then he bounded five or six paces into the street and took up his position.

'Cemil, wait!' the grocer called out after him. 'You forgot your lunch!'

'Thanks, brother,' said Cemil, and dashing back with the same exuberant step, he grabbed his sandwich and returned to his post.

The grocer noticed that the smile on the man's face did

not fade for several minutes. When he had a little free time, he took a largish piece of paper and wrote in large, neat letters:

'Our esteemed Traffic Director is seeking an assistant. Those interested are requested to apply to Mr Cemil after working hours.' He stuck it on the inside of the window so that Cemil would see it. The sign took its place above an ad that read, 'University graduate available for tutoring in maths and physics to middle and high school students.' Cemil stood up straight and tall.

No sooner had the grocer opened his shop the next day and brought in the bread and newspapers from in front of the door than Cemil entered.

'Did anybody apply for the job?' he asked excitedly.

'No, it's too soon,' replied the grocer. 'Wait a few days until people see the ad and tell their friends... There's no hurry. Somebody is bound to turn up.'

'They will tell them, won't they? There are so many people out of work,' said Cemil. 'I keep seeing them wandering around in the streets, begging. Thank God I've got a job. I'm fortunate. But I should get to my post. Just look how the cars are whizzing by.' Then he dashed into the middle of the street and took up his post. Fixing his eyes on the grocer, who was watching from the door of his shop, he gave him a crisp military salute.

The next few days were trying for the grocer. Cemil barged into the shop behind every departing customer to ask excitedly:

'Did they inquire about the ad?'

Two weeks passed and Cemil found an easy solution to the problem.

Whenever a customer left the shop, he sought out the grocer's face behind the shining lights. Raising his right arm upward and outward, he wagged his head from side to side as if to ask what happened? And the grocer in turn jerked his hand up and his head back to report 'Negative'. These signals had become almost second nature when Cemil stepped into the shop early one morning and said:

'Take the ad down. I've found a fellow. He's agreed to take the job. He'll be here today.'

The grocer was surprised.

'Really?' he asked. 'Who is it?'

'I met him yesterday. He's a poor devil. He seemed to be looking for work. I told him traffic provides the lunch and there's no salary and he accepted. He's going to come at noon. I'm going to teach him the job, don't you worry. I would never turn this place over to him without training him well.'

'Good luck with that,' muttered the grocer under his breath. 'Two hundred grams of kashar a day means five kilos a month. Oh well, I'll think of it as alms. I just hope this fool doesn't start dragging others into my shop.'

Although it was noon, no one had shown up. Shading his eyes with his hands, Cemil peered down the street from time to time. Towards the hour of the afternoon prayers he entered the grocery looking desperate.

'The poor fellow probably couldn't find the place,' he said. 'Let me eat my lunch at least. If he had come we were going to eat together. I'll have to bring him along when I come tomorrow.' Brooding and preoccupied, he waited for his sandwich. The grocer made the sandwich without saying a word, putting less kashar than usual inside the loaf of bread. Cemil took his lunch and returned to his post all agitated. Despite all his misery, he devoted his full attention to directing the traffic until 6pm. Then, leaving his post with a look of weariness on his face for the first time since he had appeared, he stepped into the grocery.

'I really wonder,' he said, 'why this boy didn't show up. I hope nothing happened to him. I'm going to find him tomorrow and bring him here. But if I'm late, take a look at the traffic now and then, will you? A red Ford with the license number DZ 300 has been passing through recently around eight in the morning. The driver is very reckless. Make sure he doesn't cause an accident. Okay, see you tomorrow. Good evening.'

Towards noon the next day, Cemil came into the grocery holding a young man by the hand.

'Look,' he said, smiling. 'This is the friend I told you about. Osman'... Then he turned affectionately to the boy.

'Look, Osman, this man is our very esteemed brother. He also fixes our lunch.'

The grocer contemplated the boy's face in horror. He was a true psycho. A filthy, slovenly, genuine nutcase with a naïve grin on his face, snot running from his nose, a wool-knit cap on his head and tattered shoes. He was probably homeless too.

Cemil pulled a handkerchief out of his pocket, wiped the boy's nose and turned to the grocer:

'Pay no mind, brother. He is going to learn. Let him sit here for now and watch me. We'll start slowly and then pick up the pace,' he said.

The grocer drew a deep breath and looked at the two of them with pity and astonishment. Then he fetched a soft drink crate, spread a thick sheet of oilcloth over it and set it outside the door of the grocery a slight distance away.

'Bring the young man over and let him sit here,' he said to Cemil, 'so he doesn't get in the way of the people going in and out. He'll be able to see you better from here.'

Cemil took the boy by the hand, brought him over and sat him down on the crate. He stuffed the handkerchief into the boy's hand.

'Wipe your nose when it runs, Osman', he said. 'or you'll turn the grocer's stomach.' Then he dashed into the middle of the street and resumed his post. From there, as if it had only just occurred to him, he called out to the grocer, who was standing in front of the door. 'Did the red Ford cause any trouble?' Then he called out to the boy: 'Watch me carefully. Don't miss any movements.'

Cemil raised his hand, waved his arm and blew his whistle until noon. He stopped the cars, then let them go, in short, he showed Osman all the fine points of his art that day. And Osman watched, sometimes Cemil, sometimes the people passing by in the street, and sometimes the flies that alighted on his knees. When his nose ran, Cemil came running. 'Wipe your nose, Osman,' he would say, taking the handkerchief from the boy's hand, wiping his nose, then thrusting the handkerchief into his hand again and dashing back to his post. When it was noon, he approached Osman looking tired but happy.

'You saw, didn't you, Osman?' he asked.

The boy grinned and wagged his head quickly from side to side a few times.

'It's not that easy, Osman,' said Cemil, drawing himself erect. 'You have to be very careful. If you aren't, there will be an accident. This is an intersection. When an accident happens, the intersection gets congested all of a sudden. Up to now I have not let a single accident happen. You too are going to learn this job.'

Osman was still wagging his head. Cemil stepped into the grocery.

'It's noon, brother. Let's have our lunch. I wonder if Traffic sent over lunch money for Osman, too?'

'They did,' said the grocer, looking very serious. Then he cut a fresh loaf in two, put a little kashar inside each half and opened two sodas.

'And this is a welcome drink for Osman from me,' he told Cemil.

'The soda is from our brother, the grocer,' Cemil whispered in Osman's ear as he handed him the sandwich and soft drink. 'Tell him thank you.'

Osman wagged his head again with the same stupid grin.

Cemil called from outside the door.

'Osman thanks you, brother.'

'You don't need to thank me.'

Cemil helped the boy eat his sandwich. He was grinning at Cemil and trying to chew at the same time. But now and then when he forgot to chew and saliva drooled down his chin from his gaping mouth, Cemil would wipe the boy's chin with the handkerchief in his hand.

'Chew!' he would say.

When the boy had eaten half the sandwich in his hand, he was full. Cemil got a piece of newspaper from the grocer, wrapped the remaining bread in it and stuck it in Osman's pocket.

'You can eat it this evening,' he said.

Then he added, 'Lunch is over, Osman. I have to get back to work. Watch closely so you learn the job quickly. Look, he admonished. We've eaten bread provided by the State. We have to earn our keep.'

Osman began howling with laughter as Cemil was returning to his post. He was laughing at Cemil's hand and arm movements.

'Don't laugh, boy. Pay attention,' Cemil shouted angrily from his post.

The boy stopped laughing and started watching.

'Look here. Over here. Don't take your eyes off me,' yelled Cemil.

When it was evening, Cemil came over to Osman. He appeared to be at the end of his tether. He took the boy by the hand and made him stand up.

'Come on,' he said, 'we're leaving. Let's go practise those movements. He wished the grocer a good evening and they started up the street.

The next morning Cemil took his place promptly at the usual hour. After glancing around for Osman, the grocer called out to Cemil:

'Good morning, Cemil. No Osman today?'

'I'll explain, brother,' replied Cemil, 'at noon...'

At noon Cemil explained while the grocer was fixing

his sandwich:

'I showed him the movements yesterday evening, but he has no ability whatsoever. You noticed too that the boy is a little crazy. More than a little actually... But still I thought he could do the job. He would have learned a trade, filled his stomach, and been of use to his people and the State. He could have learned it, too. But he's a slow boy. He learned the sign for stop. He raises his hand and holds it up, but he forgets he's got his hand in the air. If you laugh, the boy will be hurt. But the cars are not going to wait for his arm to get tired. I told him, "If it had been before, it would have been okay," I said. "There were fewer cars, life was unhurried. But this age is the age of speed." I realized that he had no intention of learning. So I said, "Don't take offence, Osman, but I'll put you in another job. Directing traffic isn't for you." Keep it in mind, brother. If you hear of any job that would suit him, let me know. You've met the boy in any case.'

The grocer nodded his head. It was all he could do to keep from laughing out loud. He gave Cemil the sandwich and Cemil thanked him. As he was going out the door, he turned back and said: 'Oh, let's put that ad up again. Maybe somebody suitable will come along.'

Translated by Virginia Taylor-Saçlıoğlu

Istanbul, Your Eyes are Black

Karin Karakaşlı

THERE ARE INFINITE instants, or instantaneous infinities. Istanbul was a sea of fireflies before her eyes. Bennu relinquished herself to the phosphorescent glow; Istanbul was telling its own story, through its flickering lights.

The city panorama framed by the window stretched out before her, a luminous river twinkling with everyone's own lies and truths. *I am waiting like I never have before – this is my truth*, the young woman thought to herself. *I am waiting for my love.* She smiled at Istanbul, winking at her in the distance.

It was no coincidence that she had moved to the top floor of this old building in a neighbourhood close to the sea. The moment she set foot in the entrance of the massive structure with its high ceiling and stone stairwell, she knew she belonged there. It was as though the delicate, engraved iron door of the lift carried its passengers not upstairs, but to another time. She had entered the flat just as the daylight began to shine down through the skylight. Then, on seeing the other shore, framed by large windows, she knew that Istanbul would be her housemate. She observed her new life companion for a long while.

The landlady, Madame Markrit, often said to her, 'Sevaçya[1] used to look at the opposite shore as well, contemplating, like you do.' She wondered why this lady, who was always very discreet with everybody else, would divulge so much about her late sister, who'd lived in this apartment for many years. Later, on seeing the black and white photos of Sevaçya in the cabinet, she understood. Frozen in those pictures was an uncanny likeness between her and this lady in her younger years. Whether it was the pearl-white skin, or the mysterious star blinking in her black eyes, she could not know, but somehow their expressions completed each other.

'The things in this cabinet are mementos from Sevaçya's girlhood. As no renter has complained up to now, I never emptied them out. Would you mind if they remained here with you?' Madame Markrit asked.

'I'm sure I'll feel better with them here,' Bennu replied. After a while, a photograph of Sevaçya came out from the cabinet and took its place in a silver frame. Sevaçya was the invisible inhabitant of the house.

Bennu always took the boat home after work in the evening, grateful to retreat to her corner without having to fight her way through a traffic jam. It allowed her some privacy in the hours before dinner. She sank deep into her burgundy coloured armchair, and in the company of her reflection in the window, she looked at Istanbul. In Istanbul, where everybody waited for who knows what and whom, she would wait for her lover, whether he arrived or not. They didn't share the same flat yet, but she started missing his presence more and more in her home. She was scared of this bond, but at the same time, recognized instinctively the thin line between solitude and independence: she longed for an independence that would not sentence her to solitude.

One night, as she was preparing the dinner table with great care as usual, the downstairs neighbour appeared at her

1. Sevaçya – Armenian word for a black-eyed woman.

door. She came with a small bowl in hand to ask for some rice. But the rice was just an excuse. Her roving eyes caught the excitement on Bennu's face and immediately focused on the table behind her. Then, taking her revenge for Bennu's half-hearted greeting, said:

'Sweetheart, it seems that I've come at the wrong moment. Do you have some rice?' Then, as she went toward the stairs, rice in hand, she made her closing attack: 'Some important advice from me to you. Don't be too kind to the men. Make yourself precious, and stay hard to get.'

Bennu's hands froze. She just stood there until the neighbour left. Then, without knowing why, she grabbed the photograph of the lovely Sevaçya and began speaking to her. In that moment it seemed as though no one else on Earth besides this woman who stepped out of time and space could really understand her.

'When I am in love, I can't play games, Sevaçya. I act as I feel. I don't feign reluctance, I love abundantly. I don't imply, I quarrel abundantly. You know, sometimes the way I am makes me feel as if I come from another planet...'

Once, Madame Markrit had said to her, smiling, 'My mama always thought that my sister came from the moon. She was an unplanned baby. In the year before her birth, we had many deaths and other troubles. It was a difficult period. We all believed that this baby would bring us better luck.'

Bennu recalled asking her, 'Her name is so melodic. What does it mean?' and she answered, 'It means, "the black-eyed one". Fits her exactly, doesn't it?' And finally, the unique tale of Sevaçya's fairytale childhood, her maiden days, poured out from the elder sister and found a new and receptive heart.

'If you asked me what's the first thing that comes to mind to describe Sevaçya, I would say a strong personality. Even as a little girl, firmly expressing what she did and didn't want, she made her choices count. Although she had many friends, sometimes she would retreat into her own world and become unreachable.'

After Madame Markrit told her that Sevaçya had received a very good education for the times and been very fond of reading, Bennu could not get out of her mind the image of this young woman excitedly going through the volumes of books in the library, many of which were in different languages. She too had a special bond with books, and knew well the isolating effect of all those volumes. A sensitive soul, having realized the vastness of life, she harboured a deep yearning for a soul-mate with whom to share this great discovery. Sevaçya had satisfied her yearning with the master jeweller Yeram, who shaped life with his craft. Yeram was a man of considerable finesse. What had most enchanted this fragile soul was his patient, caring ways and his ability to make life more beautiful.

There was a wedding photograph of them in the cabinet. Two youths, radiating a halo of light while gazing into each other's eyes. An ode to hope, they looked like heralds of joyful tidings. For this reason Bennu thought their harsh ending didn't befit their love. What business did the realities of another world have in their story? Madame Markrit's shaky voice resounded in her ears:

'I don't know, dear girl, maybe an evil eye met my black-eyed one. They were so happy, so full of tenderness. It was as if Sevaçya had found the book of her life, and Yeram the precious stone of his life. They cherished each other greatly. And then those days came and, well, what can I say...'

Madame Markrit fell silent, as if the right words for what she was about to relate did not exist in any language. Such was her silence. Bennu took the hands of this woman who had seen better days. It was a gesture of understanding. Markrit's tied up tongue unravelled with tears, cascading to a receptive ear:

'Those were the war years. All of a sudden, a special tax was levied on non-Muslims, a tax on wealth and earnings. Or should I say, a tax on poverty, my girl. The levied sums were impossible to pay. Wealth accumulated over generations was erased in one day. Our Yeram had only a small business. He had to sell all he owned to pay his debt. Then he turned his back on everything. Maybe he felt himself a stranger in his own country. He kept saying, "I didn't deserve this." One night, while Sevaçya was waiting for her husband by the window, news of his death arrived. He had collapsed on the sidewalk…'

Yeram's Stone, the book Sevaçya was writing, remained unfinished. Nobody ever saw the star in those black eyes shine again. Sevaçya would gaze out the window for long hours, quietly chatting with her Istanbul. She seemed to know that this ancient city understood her, and had proven her existence by rendering her so much pain. These chats continued until one ruthless autumn.

'It was 1955. Tensions were high because of the events in Cyprus. News spread that somebody had put a bomb in Ataturk's birth house in Thessaloniki. A raging crowd turned Istanbul to hell that night. The whole affair was later uncovered to be a plot, but what does that matter now? Churches, houses and shops of non-Muslims burnt to the ground… Most of all, our hearts were burning. They came in front of our house too. We watched them from behind this tulle curtain. One voice shouted: "Whoever loves Mohammed, show us the houses of the infidels!" There was silence for a moment. Then, we heard the roaring voice of our neighbour, Mr. Muammer. "This is a Muslim neighbourhood, none of the kind you speak of can be found here."'

The flaming horror of that night was visible on Madame Markrit's face. 'That is the way it was, my girl. This neighbour saved us. Later, he came to our house with his wife and we hugged each other. He couldn't look into our eyes, as if he himself were to blame. Sevaçya said to him, "You are our brother." This big man then started to weep like a child…'

Madame Markrit slowly turned her hands that had

THE BOOK OF ISTANBUL

dropped into her lap. She spoke to her palms about a night that had never turned into a memory, but remained forever in the present. 'Do you know what happened then, my girl? All of a sudden, Sevaçya pushed the window open wide. Looking at the destruction, she shouted, so loud as if tearing her lungs to pieces: "*Bolis, hokis... Bolis, hokis...*" She was saying, "Istanbul my love, Istanbul my soul …"'

Again Bennu was rooted to her armchair. That voice rang in her ears. Right on this night, when the man she loved was so late… The arms of the clock chilled the blood in her veins. Something must have happened… Just as when Sevaçya was eating her heart out for her love and her Istanbul. Still no news from the awaited one… The mobile phone kept repeating the same refrain: 'The number you have dialled can not be reached at this time. Please try again later.'

She pressed her forehead on the cool glass. Her eyes fixed on the hospital nearby. Who knows who awaits death in that place, their loved ones seeking consolation in vain. Then she thought about prisons where there was no escape, drinking houses where each table tells of another facet of life, miserable hotels of the exiled, dwellings that never become homes, where people are forced to live, still called Istanbul but miles from the city. The young woman took a deep breath. Istanbul crept inside her. The weight of the city pressed on her heart.

That sound whirring in her ear… the doorbell. How far from the window to the door, from life to death, how long a step to take… There he was, on the threshold. The man she loved was speaking to her, 'My love, the traffic was so bad, I was delayed and my phone battery ran out of charge. I am so sorry.' He was about go on explaining, but stopped. Right then, the young woman jumped from death to life in his arms and wept several lifetimes. She couldn't embrace this body, this soul tightly enough. Suddenly the man held her face in his hands, looked at her a long time and said, 'Marry me.' The woman raised her palms to his cheeks and said, 'I will!' He kissed the tears in her eyes, the smile on her face. They remained in a long embrace. Sevaçya was smiling to the lovers, smiling to life from her photograph in black and white.

Translated by Carol Yürür

I Did Not Kill Monsieur Moise

Mario Levi

MONSIEUR DE TOLEDO liked dozing off while listening to Mozart, and often drinking wine to ease his solitude. If you saw him in his armchair, lost in one of those naps, you would have thought, *how defenceless and withdrawn he seems in his little world.* That he knew Edith Piaf when she was but a smutty street singer in Menilmontant, that he could recall with great excitement and in the least expected moments a love affair from years ago in Berlin, that his young heart had been an involuntary witness to the rise of fascism in Rome, that he had exchanged greetings – albeit from a distance and somewhat secretly – with Trotsky during his days in Büyükada, that, past the age of forty, he had gone to Aşkale to break rocks, or that he had been engaged on four separate occasions – none of this you would have guessed, much less imagined. The odour around the room, the general decay, his very idiosyncratic solitude – not unlike all serious cases of solitude – might have led you to sense, at the most, the inconveniences of a very long and exhausting life. You might have observed this nap like you would an unforeseen storm, and found it altogether difficult to understand how someone who had lived so fully and known so many, could make do with so few words. Furthermore, you might have appeared before me with a smile on your face and some of your own opinions on the matter, and, although I would have preferred otherwise, you might even have been correct. But, believe me, this would not be the end of it. Because, not just in this particular mystery, but in nearly every prevarication in his life, Monsieur Moise proved surprising. To appreciate fully the significance of this fact, one has to be not only an Istanbul Jew but also a dreamer of small dreams, an expert in defeats, and most importantly, a champion of rehearsals and self-deception. For instance, he had never been able to deceive a woman, never been able to steal someone else's ideas, always strived to be keenly literate, but, in contrast to some who excelled in writing, he spent too much time reading to ever find the time to become a writer. He always enjoyed travelling, and although he was of a respectable age and entitled to a degree of indifference, he never managed to rid himself of the dread of coming back, and especially after being forced into certain dead-ends, he preferred to always stay in familiar surroundings and among familiar people. I remember him saying, 'I ought to write the ode to postponement.' Believe me, he would have easily succeeded in writing it, for he was the very embodiment of postponement. Yet I think you, too, will recognize what an impossible dead-end it is to suspend so many longings in the name of quotidian consolations.

When I think about all this, despite the objections of my feelings, my strange habits, my nerves and – quite incredibly to most of you – my good intentions, and at the risk of upsetting some of my faithful companions in life's journey, in the end I have to say that Monsieur Moise was our odd 'neighbour' who had, as they say, lost his compass. It wasn't because he had inadvertently sidestepped the Tahtakale-Şişli[1] orbit or because he had once said that during Passover one could eat matzo between slices of bread, but, as I see it, his congeniality – which could go head-to-head with his oddness – had to do with the fact that year after year on Christmas Eve he brought a bouquet of carnations to a certain 'Marika' whom we never saw, and that – in sharp contrast with his quotidian life – he made companions

1. Tahtakale-Şişli – The city quarter where Jewish people typically lived.

among the literary heroes in his library to whom he could pour out his heart almost anytime. Insecurity. The fear of getting lost unexpectedly in the increasingly altered, lifeless, unwelcoming, unquestioning human cangıl[2]. The longing to retreat into the silences, into his alcohol solitude. To take refuge in them, perhaps for entire nights, along with his illusions, misperceptions and defeats. I think this longing is what kept us from learning right away that, on his last evening, he had prepared for himself a fine feast of *menemen* and wine.

'He must have died at least three days ago,' my editor said on the evening of the day when we, with aching sadness in our hearts, went to pay our respects to the deceased. His body had been growing cold for some time. 'Shame, what a shame!' he said, adding, 'He was about to accept that Dmitry isn't as bad as everyone assumes he is.'

'Let it be,' I said. 'At any rate, it was to be expected. Whether or not we want to, aren't we always late?'

Late for a person, a possibility or the appearance of mutual understanding… Yes, always late in arriving, never quite getting there. Perhaps now I will have to rethink the implications these words might evoke. After all, some might even say that Monsieur Moise's death was overdue, that, in these strange days of ours, his cold body had arrived late among us, that once again our timing was off in receiving each other's news. Regardless, the deceased looked as though he had a vague, indistinct smile on his face that morning, he still had wine in his glass, his watch was still running, right next to him there was the faded photograph of a woman whose true story very few people knew, and he had scribbled on a tiny piece of paper – maybe very shortly before dying – a sentence like, 'You shouldn't have trapped me inside these four walls and my hopes.' Right then my whole being was filled with a bittersweet happiness that I still find difficult to describe; it was the kind of happiness that germinates in the

2. cangıl – Jungle, transliterated from English to Turkish.

heart as if in another form, something akin to a very meaningful sorrow, the kind that spins and weaves its own pain and consequences. Because, to me, this tiny sentence seemed to put into words – quite unexpectedly – a struggle that had been carried out for many years and with some degree of resignation and conscious self-deception. Monsieur Moise, in a manner of speaking, had scored a last-minute goal.

As for his funeral… We didn't exactly make a crowd as we accompanied him on his last journey on Earth. Of course it was not surprising that we felt an obligation and suffered its bittersweet taste. Monsieur Moise was one of those people who asked questions more often than he received answers, and who often rowed his boat against the current and never quite acknowledged it; after all, he was among those who ran around like a crazy goat in the days when so many of the sentiments he cherished, the values he staunchly held, were being debated and increasingly judged in the vocabulary of a habitual consensus held by his obligatory friends.

Worse yet, despite the persistent struggle that lasted a lifetime; the ideas defended year after year in this struggle; the price paid – willingly or not – for those ideas; despite the long-settled preferences of the deceased and our most forcefully voiced objections, this funeral, too, like all other funerals, included a religious service. Uncertain of the fact yet willing to corroborate certain rumours, we even claimed that the deceased had committed suicide, but to no avail. To add insult to injury, the prayers were said in Hebrew. Had he been able to raise his head, as it were, Monsieur Moise would have had difficulty following the last earthly ceremony being performed on his behalf. Still, we opted for our customary – and by now quite wearisome – response to situations of helplessness, telling each other, 'In the end, these are merely details; let's attend to what really matters.'

However, among the details, there was one that I must mention to you: a woman, her tired image, her evocative features, or the impression such features left on me, none of which can be easily shared with someone else. A woman who stood at a distance, conscientiously dressed in black, her face covered with a black veil, a woman who unexpectedly sprang from the past, ushering with her the hints and possibilities of a story experienced a long time ago, and all the memories she stirred or intended to stir… When I singled her out like this – and for no legitimate reason – I somehow recalled that icy evening wind on Sıracevizler Street; the little indiscretions, the hours at the piano, the three-storey building with the garden on Izzetpasa Street, the questions, the letters, the unsayables, the journeys toward a possibility, growing old among the books, the *tête-à-têtes*, the instances of helplessness postponed, the story I had been trying to write for years, its history within me; the way I had tried to ask again certain questions, without thinking about their answers. If somehow I forced the traces of disjointed memories, I could perhaps resuscitate some of the missing feelings and images, set them back into place, and all of a sudden complete the narrative arc. Yet for the time being, I was satisfied thinking that the woman might be the same one in the faded photograph.

But was this a misperception, albeit perfectly reasonable and defensible? Unfortunately, I will never be able to answer this question. Because everything now rests behind a veil of imagination, as if to justify my memory of her. Still, whatever the actual fact may be, I like to believe that our unexpected visitor was involved in some way, and no doubt Monsieur Moise would have derived great joy from her visit.

As we were leaving the cemetery, my editor said pretty much the same thing: 'Of all the capable writers, we ended up with the ones who can only describe those people.' He was right. Monsieur Moise ought to have realized that he had a writer hidden in him, I thought to myself. Because writing could provide a little consolation, a reassuring delay on the journey toward a contradiction, toward a categorical indescribability. But wasn't publishing what one wrote another form of reconciliation, and therefore compromise? I don't believe Monsieur Moise considered this question in the midst of all the turmoil. We may still keep in mind that certain stories will engender other stories in us; that, whether or not we want to, we will be forced at times to heed the call of seasons changing, owing to the sorrow that can run endlessly inside us; that, in other words, in certain relationships we will always leave behind parts of ourselves, our deaths.

Let's say an entirely different road stretches ahead of you. And that's when – no matter what your journey or your likely return may promise – you search for a word, a word that, despite everything, has not been worn out or depleted. A word or a certain restless sensation – that, by now, feels familiar, almost second-nature – a rehearsal of an inner monologue. Can you ever risk another exchange like this?

Translated by Aron R. Aji

A Panther

Özen Yula

IT WAS A panther, slinking slowly down the avenue. With a syncopated stride it prowled through the night. Three-thirty in the morning. All was very quiet. An atmosphere of prayer beads and the smoldering ash of hookahs mingled with burnt wood. There were none who understood why their sweethearts were asleep far from them at this hour. There were many men with broken hearts – and many women – but no one died of a broken heart. They all suffered together. There were many loves estranged from one another. The panther didn't realize this. No panther can converse in words. Wild, black and beautiful, it can rend the night asunder.

This panther's life in the jungle was long gone. Too far away for refuge, much too distant to reach. Those old days were like this city. As the animal had never been downtown before, it didn't know its way. All doors were locked at night in this new city. Bitter victuals, grime, and a stinking sanctified garden was what the panther knew here. It had viewed this world only from its hiding-place behind a tree. Dismal people would come to stop and stare, long and hard, at the animal. Those human beings fond of speaking to one-another inside doorways when they visited each another, fond of gossip and always hesitant to say their good-byes. The panther stared backed at them without sympathy or understanding. Understanding, after all, might prevent it from doing them in. This failure in comprehension was what was best for a panther. The animal would observe these people and when one caught his fancy, would make a sudden leap. Sometimes it would hurt its head, banging hard against the intervening iron bars. Then those outside the cage would retreat in horror. That is to say, not just stepping back, but outright fleeing – sometimes not even bothering to look behind them. They loved such panic. That way they'd have something to tell their neighbours about – and later their grandchildren. They wouldn't let their children go up close. They were well aware that a close encounter would immediately mature a child; the child would cease to be a child. To quash their fright, the children would suddenly grow up. Such children no longer loved their parents. What people fear the most is the loss of their children's love. For in their old age, they'd have no one to take care of them.

Right now night was falling – upon the sea, the ferries, the bridges and the streets all covered with snow. At night a panther's teeth gleam. Like a poem roams the panther through the night.

Dragging one hind leg, the panther trusts its instinct and proceeds as quickly as possible, still agile – if not as much as before.

Across the snow, one poor soul spies a huge object swiftly heading straight towards him. Gigantic and pitch black in the predawn of a snowy white morn. His last glimpse is that of sharp claws and teeth piercing his flesh and his eyes. His last sensation, that of a weight painfully crashing onto his chest. In place of his last breath only a whisper escapes his lips. Only with difficulty can the poor man gasp one last breath through his nose. This breath is lost, lingering deep inside, as the panther snatches a huge mouthful of his face. Left starving for three days. The food the animal devoured a short while ago had hardly begun to fill his belly.

The humans who'd arrived at the garden uninvited three days ago had sorely tested the panther's patience. They'd screamed constantly. It was one of the sunniest days of the whole winter. The garden was overrun with children. Before the end of term someone had decided to bring the pupils to the Zoological Garden. Of course there'd been some parents not overly pleased about this, but their objections were feeble. Two days later, there were the children shouting and shrieking as they looked at the animals in the Zoological Garden. All the children were excited. Children can be cruel and they can be naïvely innocent. These were of an age where cruelty predominated.

They were yelling at the top of their lungs. One quiet puny boy held back from the crowd and gazed continuously at the panther's cage. He displayed an independence from the jostling mass, and bore the unusual poise of belonging anywhere and everywhere. His day would come, sometime in his life; that day he'd have to go, that he *would* go – perversely, without so much as a backward glance. In his wake he'd leave some crying, perhaps some longing for his return. He'd pay no heed. Understanding that the world was indeed a rather small sphere, every explanation naught but a tall tale, the boy would go. Like a poem, like a quatrain, like a proud but weary stray bitch on the street.

Not understanding this of course, the panther looked on. Deadly as a violent passion. The children were screaming and jostling, their teachers paying no attention. Life was quiet, voices were loud, the children were nasty. They would never quite be able to remember whose idea it had been, once they'd grown up (because it's only human nature to share blame and fault, living more comfortably by always interpreting what others have done as worse than one's own deeds, tending to see, to find, to analyze it thus), but someone among them gave a signal to the others. All of them ran – as spiritedly, joyously and happily as if watching a cartoon – and lifted the boy, to heave him up into the air straight toward the panther's cage. His puny frame teetered once or twice atop the bars before he plunged down on the other side.

The boy uttered no sound. Leaping upon him at lightening speed, the panther sank its teeth into his throat and the boy breathed his last. Neither a tear nor a scream. The children stared at their friend, instantaneously turned to blood and flesh. One or two nervous giggles broke an all-encompassing silence. Then a little girl's shriek rent the air; the teachers began to throw up and the children ran away. With great appetite, its front legs planted upon the child, the panther began to tear huge chunks off the boy's frame. By the time the keeper arrived, it had devoured nearly two thirds of the child.

Immediately they beat the panther and as further punishment left it hungry for the next three days. Every now and then the keeper would enter the cage, a long iron staff in hand, to land a firm blow somewhere upon the panther's body. This hurt the panther very much. As the animal roared and leapt at the keeper, the man would instantly disappear through the hole by which he'd entered. With all its strength, the panther would then throw itself against the door. With its coat of black satin rippling over its taut muscles, the panther adopted one stance after another. One new pose after another filled its skin. Its frame was overflowing with panthers. An urge for revenge was swelling inside. It nurtured a terrible anger in its eyes. Some things a panther cannot hide; cannot hide even should it want to. It was filled with the urge to kill. Sensing this urge from the animal's behaviour, the keeper remained on the alert for an attack, and with his years of experience, each time easily succeeded in retreating safely. He struck it powerfully, with blows not quite hard enough to break its bones. The blows were carefully measured. Certainly they didn't want to lose the panther. It brought good money to the Zoological Garden. The monkeys, the snakes, the alligators, and then the panther. The number of paying visitors reflected such a preference.

Because the boy who died came from a poor family, no ruckus was raised. There was no need to put the panther to sleep. The veterinarian decided it would be better to take it off its food for a while and teach it a lesson. The news made one or two papers and appeared five or six times on television, to whet people's appetites and to dull their memory of the tax-evasion lawsuit pending against the zoo managers. Within two or three days, however, the managers had been cleared of the charges by their friends and accomplices in Parliament; the television then played down the event and played up the completely new tack of what a wonderful and outstanding management was running the zoo, serving their country cleanly and honestly. Thus a frosted glass was drawn across the images of the impoverished child and his tearful family and the pieces of flesh left behind; like faded pictures, these had been relegated to the recycling bins in the memories of the country's citizens.

Life would have continued peacefully in the Zoological Garden. Only, last night the keeper made a mistake. His eyes weren't what they used to be. He pushed the door part-way open and slipped into the panther's cage. The fluorescent lamp in the garden was hardly enough to light the cage well. The man proceeded slowly towards the panther's lair. He pointed the iron rod in his hand towards the mouth of the lair. The iron rod was ready and waiting for the panther to emerge. Crouched in another corner of the cage, the panther squinted its eyes, assessing the situation. The darkest corner of the cage was now blacker than black. By the time the keeper sensed the sudden motion behind him, it was much too late. Screams echoed through the darkness of the night. As the keeper breathed his last, the panther was taking out its wrath on his stringy meat, after being starved for days on end. The blood draining from the man reached the edge of the cage and began to drip out into the garden. The soil was imbibing his blood. Consuming first the neck, then the kidneys and part of the man's back, the panther had sated its hunger somewhat. Now it was time for action.

With one forepaw it pushed the door wide open and with a finesse hardly to be expected from that huge body, it flowed through the doorframe like water. By the laws of nature the panther was a killer. Nature was founded on killing. Animals and people killed one another, sometimes even themselves. God, then, killed them all. According to the concepts of the age, people were also doing away with God. At night, on television screens, they would gaze at the Iraqis killed by American mercenary soldiers. God, with each dying child, was dying once again with the conscience of the age. That night, the panther escaped from the cage in which it had, for long years, been held hostage.

Coal-black upon the white snow. Shimmering black satin in the blackness of the night. It climbed onto a rise overlooking the spiky iron pickets of a garden fence. It placed its forefeet on the pedestal of a metal statue there. Braced by its strong hind legs, it hurled itself upward, toppling the metal figurine of the statue into the falling snow.

The panther hung motionless for an instant, arched in the air like a billow of velvet. If anyone had been there to witness it, they could have testified that time froze like a single frame in a paused film.

As its front paws landed on the snow-covered, stone-paved road outside the garden, its entire body was wrenched. The snow broke its fall somewhat. But with the blow of its hind legs striking the ground, the panther was stunned for a moment and sank to the ground. Snow clung to its fur. Worse than the cold, though, was the shock from the impact. The panther could sense the need to quickly move on from where it was. It made one or two attempts to get to its feet. It couldn't yet stand up. It would have to wait for a while. Being unable to rise when it wanted frustrated the panther. Certain animals and certain people should die before they grow old. Before their bodies fail them, before they lose the ability to move about exactly when they want and how they want. The panther didn't know this. There was only a strange stiffness in its body. Something it had never known, never felt before. A little later the panther would move on, but there was a terrific pain in its back leg. It hurt badly.

In the forest, indeed anywhere in life, a crippled panther

has scant chance of survival. More than chance was needed now.

It had been snowing all day, and Istanbul had turned into a pure white sculpture. All the dirt, all the filth, all the evil was blanketed; a city worth living in had sprung up. Nearly everyone was at home. The ferryboat service connecting the two shores had long since shut down. At one point the fog crept in, and when it rose, it left a city masterfully wrapped in a snow-white cloak.

Later, as the snow abated, people were snug at home, the city silent. It was the first time this terrible city had ever looked so safe. Nighttime – and Istanbul an ice sculpture. If you could only reach out your hand, the minarets of Hagia Sophia would snap at the flick of your finger. That icy – the moon, cruel, a crescent of glass. This much nature bereft of the populace was as touching as it was beautiful, but still there was a chill in the air. An atmosphere, a signal, a sign.

The hour for roasting chestnuts over the stove was long past. That night the radiators stayed warm. The children had drunk their warm milk and gone to bed. The lights in the homes were all turned off. But those not sleepy, the sleepless, those who never sleep were still chasing after another life. They were pursuing the lifestyles they believed would make them happy.

Snow is again drifting slowly, slowly down over Istanbul. Fluffy flakes, brightening the night as though dawn were approaching, swirl and drift aimlessly along. The flakes fall on the panther's coat. Each snowflake trembling where it alights upon on the fur. Twitching and pitching like whitecaps, it turns the panther's body into a fantasy of open sea. Shivering, the animal rises to its feet. Its hind leg is still very painful. The panther, an animal accustomed to expressing its grief in sound, is remarkably quiet. As if aware what would happen if it should howl just now. At the police station nearby, life is still in motion. Drunks, troublemakers, those who could not make it home, and the bleary-eyed staff.

As the snowfall grows more intense, it falls upon the left-over meat of the keeper. Life, at that moment, resembled a sacrificial ritual revived from antiquity. But the blood has long been covered by the snow. The soil and the snow share the blood between themselves. The panther, at one side of the avenue, is making its way uphill along the sidewalk. It senses that any sudden movement would magnify the pain. With a delicate gait, it tries to flow along the avenue into the night.

There's not a soul on the avenue, in the streets. The ATM shelters are filled with glue-sniffers, with the homeless. Their reeking bodies – if unaware of their own stinking blight, only too conscious of their dire fright – huddle arm-in-arm. Some luckier ones, running across temporary soup kitchens set up for those caught out by the snow, have now swallowed a cup of hot mush as a substitute for soup and after a few puffs on a cigarette drifted off to sleep. But in the city there are also those taking refuge behind locked doors in apartments with heated floors; those who, having left their worries outside, have watched one of those programmes of 'real life recorded 24/7' aimed at their own class, and are now sleeping comfortably.

An elderly woman who can't sleep, gazing out the window of her ground floor apartment, catches sight of a coal-black creature passing by outside. This creature's coming at a run, stirring up the snow and scattering it to either side. Something seems to be amiss with one of its feet, but it's still moving apace. The woman's dry and aging old lips suddenly stir, mouthing syllable after syllable. She's reciting an archaic prayer – neither *of* her own, nor *in* her own language – that she'd once been taught. In hope of help from a God who long, long ago descended onto the earth only to have been forgotten. Then, as fast as her aged and weary body can move she goes straight for her mobile phone. Now she's busy trying to find her son's number on the phone, a present from her daughter-in-law who had recorded the number 'just in case.'

She pushes one key and the number's dialled automatically.

As the panther presses on through the night, the sleepy state employee at the other end of the line is straining hard to understand what the elderly lady is going on about.

The road was winding uphill. The panther was in much greater pain now because more weight fell upon its hind legs. A roar rumbled through the night. A hoarse but strong voice slipping among the snowflakes, reverberating halfway up the slope. Then it faded from earshot under a thick layer of snow. To stay on the safe side, the stray dogs in the streets curled up more tightly where they were and made no sound at all.

The growls did not cease, but followed one after another. Until the panther reached the top of the hill, it released the brunt of its pain through its throat. The howl of the blowing snow at least took the edge off these complaints. In the dreams of those deep asleep, a jungle documentary began to play. As for the drunkards, they simply concluded that the dogs in the city had been thrown somewhat off kilter.

Toward the top of the slope the panther spied a taxi driver ensconced in his taxi. He was deep asleep. Passing the car, the animal stopped in the middle of the now nearly level road. The snow suddenly let up. Everything was peaceful. The whole city resembled a cake of ice, frosted with powdered sugar. The panther paused. It assessed its pain.

The poor driver decided to take advantage of the let-up in the snow to step outside his tin prison. Inhaling the fresh coolness of predawn, he could leisurely smoke a cigarette. Like he used to do when he was in the army. It would do him good after the rakı he'd drunk. He stretched. Crackling sounds came from his joints. These he heard; these sounds that pervaded his body were nothing if not a curse at life. On the snow in front of him, then, he spied a strange creature. He must have seen the likes of it in films. It looked like a predatory beast. As if mesmerized, he watched each movement of the animal. His still unlit cigarette fell from his hand.

The panther didn't want to carry the rest of the repast along with it. To protect the kill, though, to show other predators and scavengers that this meat had an owner, would have been the animal's normal behaviour. But now, carrying the meat would slow it down. Now it had to be on its way; it had to return to where it belonged. It licked the blood from its face and claws. Then it moved on.

Quickly, it proceeded up the avenue. Just below its neck there remained some dried blood from the poor man. The panther wasn't going to clean it off.

Moving rapidly along the level avenue, there, just ahead to the right, it glimpsed what it was looking for. A woeful roar issued from its throat. The pain had now become unbearable.

When the remains of the keeper's body were discovered at the Zoological Garden, all hell broke loose. Finding it difficult to follow the footprints of the panther, the authorities began to evaluate the clues they had. The animal couldn't have gone far. The old woman's telephone call headed them in the right direction. Rifles in hand, marksmen were spreading out along the avenue, and police had been stationed at each corner. The streets and avenues were alight with the constantly rotating lights on the roofs of the police cars. Blue followed by red, then blue, then red again. İstiklal Caddesi had been cordoned off. The panther strolled alone down the middle of the avenue. It moved along right above the tram tracks. Suddenly it quickened its pace.

The first marksman to spot the running animal pointed it out to his teammate, warmly wrapped in a padded anorak. The excitement and exhaustion, the distress and cold shivers down his spine that he knew from the days... months... years ... of military service in the Southeast returned to him. With mixed feelings he raised his rifle and concentrated on focusing on the black object opposite him. At that moment he was gripped only by the need to destroy the enemy before him. All his humanity was automatically switched off. What he saw at that moment was the enemy scurrying in and out of the rocks under the scorching sun of a south-eastern afternoon.

The panther was running faster and faster. Ahead of him, men in heavy coal-black garb lifted their rifles in aim. They would inflict pain. Just the keeper had done. Pain that would set his soul alight.

At any rate, the panther now had a goal in sight. A bit further ahead – but much closer than where those black men were standing – that old life was calling out from a shop window. On a huge screen, the jungle was shining and shimmering. Colors that the animal could not make out, but forms that were familiar: signs of his former existence there in the window. There were parrots flying about, scarcely visible beneath the luxuriant foliage. The camera was wandering between the tree trunks. Creatures of the forest scattered to the left and right.

As quickly as possible the panther planted all its weight on its hind legs, tensed, and sprung with all its might straight at the window. What it wanted, what it longed for, what it remembered, was right there behind the glass. Its most bitter roar yet rent the air. The pain in its hind leg was horrendous.

Glowing, a red-hot shot of metal pierced the predawn darkness. The bullet was flying straight on target. With remarkable speed the panther leapt through the glass. This was an act the marksman was not prepared for. The window splintered and shattered. The bullet whisked past its target. The only sound it made was a whistle. The panther, its coat suddenly bathed in blood from the shards, sailed directly into the flat screen of the giant television. Its body was shaken by the full impact of the electric current. Bombs burst in its body, earthquakes rumbled, fires broke out. Only one horrific roar. Blood, blackness, the dismal break of day.

Red, yellow, blue, green and bright white lights lit up the darkness. The sharpshooters opposite gazed into a veritable kaleidoscope.

Another television in the back of the shop was broadcasting pictures of American soldiers killing Iraqi civilians. There was an immediate change of scene. Bombs appeared raining down upon Iraq during the night. Fireworks burst in the Iraqi night. Now and then explosions could be seen. Torment masterfully caught in visual images. In terror, the people there had disappeared somewhere beneath the city. The people in this city, though, were sound asleep.

The panther landed in a small clearing of the jungle that had been visible on the screen, surrounded by tall majestic trees. Tall grasses tenderly swathed its body. Its hind leg felt better. Scenes of youthful play – its struggling to clamber onto its mother's back – passed one by one through its memory. It remembered that the jungle was infinite.

The traces of blood beneath its mouth had vanished.

It was no longer growling in pain.

It was a panther.

Fast, black, gliding along in harmony with nature.

A crystal clear sky was beginning to dawn over snow-covered Istanbul.

Newspapers were being delivered to homes.

The city was awakening.

Cracklings could be heard in the frosted cake of ice.

Translated by Jean Carpenter Efe

Contributors

Türker Armaner (b. 1968) holds a PhD in philosophy from Saint-Denis University, Paris. He has taught at many universities in Istanbul and is currently a full-time instructor at the Philosophy Department of Galatasaray University. As a literary author and an academic, Armaner has published three collections of short stories and novellas, *Kıyısız* (Without A Coast), *Taş Hücre* (The Stone Cell), *Dalgakıran* (Breakwater), and recently a novel, *Tahta Saplı Bıçak* (The Knife With A Wooden Handle).

Murat Gülsoy's works explore the metafictional potential of self-consciousness with 'page-turning' plots. Besides short stories, he has written four books addressing modern masters Kafka, Borges, Eco, Stern, Fowles and Orhan Pamuk. *Stehlen Sie dieses Buch* was the first of his books to be translated into German, and his novel inspired from Max Ernst's collages, *A Week of Kindness in Istanbul*, has been translated to Chinese, Macedonian, Romanian, and Bulgarian.

Nedim Gürsel was born in Gaziantep, Turkey, in 1951. The 1971 coup d'etat led to his exile in France, where he studied at the Sorbonne. One of Turkey's most celebrated authors, he faced trial in 2009 for 'denigrating religious values' in his novel, *The Daughters of Allah*, which was also awarded the Freedom of Expression and Publishing Award. His short story collection *Son Tramvay* (The Last Tram) will be published in English translation by Comma Press in 2011.

Muge İplikci made her name with the short story collections *Perende* (Somersault), *Columbus'un Kadınları* (Columbus' Women), *Arkası Yarın* (To Be Continued) and *Transit Yolcular* (Transit Passengers). Her latest collection of short stories, *Kısa Ömürlü Açelyalar* (Azaleas), was published in 2010. She's also written two novels, *Kül ve Kel* (The Ash and Wind) in 2004, *Cemre* (The Harbinger) in 2006 and *Kafdağı* (Mount Kaf) in 2008

CONTRIBUTORS

Karin Karakaşlı was born in Istanbul in 1972. From 1996 to 2006 she was a senior editor at the Turkish-Armenian weekly newspaper *Agos*, and a columnist for its Turkish and Armenian sections. Her books include the short story collections *Başka dillerin şarkısı* (Songs in Other Languages) and *Can Kırıkları* (Splinters of the Heart), a novel, *Müsait bir yerde inebilir miyim* (Can I Get Off At The Next Stop?), and the poetry collection *Benim Gönlüm Gümüş* (My Heart is of Silver). She is a columnist at *Radikal 2* newspaper.

Sema Kaygusuz (b. 1972) continues to draw inspiration from the wide range of folk tales, legends, and stories she collected during her rural childhood. In 1997, her first book of short stories, *Ortadan Yarısından* (Straight Through the Heart) was published. The next, *Sandık Lekesi* (Chest Stain), won the Cevdet Kudret Literature Prize, followed by *Doyma Noktası* (Saturation Point) and *Esir Sözler Kuyusu* (The Well of Captive Utterances). In 2006, Kaygusuz co-authored the award-winning screenplay *Pandora's Box* with Yeşim Ustaoğlu.

Gönül Kıvılcım has lived in Berlin and Cologne, working for the German television network WDR and the Turkish newspaper *Radikal*. Her first book, a collection of short stories called *A Small Town and Lies*, was published in 2001 and translated into German. Her other books are *Razor Boy* (Can, 2002), *Fragmented Loves* (Everest, 2004) and *Karakoy Through Living Witnesses* (Heyamola, 2009).

Mario Levi was born in 1957 in Istanbul. His first short story collection, *Bir Şehre Gidememek* (Unable to go to the City) won the Haldun Taner Story Prize. A year later, he published his second collection, *Madam Floridis Dönmeyebilir* (Madam Floridis May Not Return), which focused on the lives of minorities living in Istanbul. His novel *İstanbul Bir Masaldı* (Istanbul Was a Fairy Tale) won the Yunus Nadi Novel Prize in 2000. His latest novel *Karanlık Çökerken Neredeydiniz?* (Where Were You When Darkness Fell?) was published in 2009.

Özen Yula's first collection of short stories, *Öbür Dünya Bilgisi* (Knowledge from the Other World) was published in 1993. His plays have been translated to English, German, French, Italian, Finnish, Polish, Bulgarian, Bosnian, Japanese and Arabic. His recent play, *Yala Ama Yutma* (Lick but Don't Swallow), caused a national controversy before it opened in Istanbul in 2010. An exploration of women's rights and social justice, it was condemned by the fundamentalist press.

Mehmet Zaman Saçlıoğlu is a prolific short story writer. His third collection, *Ruzgar Geri Getirirse* (If The Wind Brings It Back, sub-titled: Stories With Thresholds), was published in 2002. Examining themes of fear, punishment, reward, love, and duty, his collections are considered among the best examples of contemporary short story writing in Turkey. *If The Wind Brings it Back* was published in Hungary in 2008 by Napkut Kiado under the title *Ha Visszahozza a szel*.

Translators

Aron R. Aji is a dean at St. Ambrose University, Davenport, Iowa, USA. A native of Turkey, he has translated fiction, poetry and plays by Turkish writers into English. His translation of Bilge Karasu's *The Garden of Departed Cats* (New Directions) won the 2004 National Translation Award. Aji also received a 2006 National Endowment for the Arts fellowship for his current translation project, another novel by Karasu, *The Evening of a Very Long Day*.

Jean Carpenter Efe (d. 2008) was a teacher and translator with a specific interest in archeology. Amongst her many published translations are *Archaeological Survey in the Harran Plain* and *The Salvage Excavations at Orman Fidanlığı*. She also co-edited *Tales from the Taurus*, the collected stories of Osman Şahin.

Ruth Christie's previous translations include *In the Temple of a Patient God*, by Bejan Matur, a major collection poems by Oktay Rifat (with Richard McKane) and *The Shelter Stories* of Feyyaz Kayacan Fergar.

CONTRIBUTORS

Amy Spangler's many published translations include *The City in Crimson Cloak* by Aslı Erdoğan (Soft Skull Books, New York) and *Gallipoli, 1915: Through Turkish Eyes* by Haluk Oral (İş Bankası Yayınları, Istanbul). She's the editor of *Istanbul Noir* (Akashic Books, New York) and founder of the Anatolialit agency.

Carol Stevens Yürür is a translator, academic and editor. Two of her translations of Mehmet Zaman Saçlıoğlu short stories have previously been published in English language anthologies in England and Turkey.

Virginia Taylor-Saçlıoğlu's literary translations have appeared in *An Anthology of Modern Turkish Short Stories*, edited by Fahir Iz (Bibliotheca Islamica, Chicago) and in *Nar '96* edited by Saliha Paker (Oğlak Yayınları, Istanbul).

Ruth Whitehouse has a PhD in Modern Turkish Literature at the School of Oriental and African Studies. She's worked as a translator from Turkish and Persian into English since 1999, and in 2009, participated in the Cunda Translation Workshop at Ayvalik, Turkey.

Special Thanks

The editors and publishers would like to thank TEDA, the Turkish Translation Subvention Programme; David Codling of the British Council in Istanbul; The Cunda International Workshop for Translators of Turkish Literature; Nermin Mollaoğlu and the Kalem Literary Agency; Amy Spangler and the Anatolialit Literary Agency; Müge Sökmen at Metis Books; Saliha Paker of Boğaziçi University Istanbul; Abdullah Pehlivan at the London Business Guide; Arts Council England; and the Pasha Hotel, London.